The Glass Heart

REDEEMED HEARTS COLLECTION
BOOK ONE

LC TAYLOR

Chapter One

IT FEELS like being trapped inside a maze with no exit as Jesse stared at the mounds and mounds of boxes mocking her from their perch on the floor. Who'd of thought two people could have so much crap between them...? She didn't realize they'd accrued this much stuff. But sitting on the floor staring at the contents of their life together felt suffocating.

How was she supposed to unpack everything alone? Jesse wasn't sure she wanted to open Pandora's box and let herself feel the pain tucked away in corrugated traps. The thought crossed her mind several times to take everything to the dump and start over fresh without remembering what once was.

Her well-thought-out life had been reduced to a couple of dozen boxes. It's all she had left of what she thought would be forever. Trinkets, pictures, and clothes of the man she loved—but not him. A military widow at her age felt monumental... Only twenty-six fucking years old, and she'd already buried her heart. A heart stolen in the dead of night. The energy Jesse needed to make the place livable was gone and buried six feet beneath the cold earth—where the legless creatures roamed—the black, dirty space home to her husband.

Alex had just turned thirty when his life was snuffed out.

He had so much to give to the world—and that's what he did. Only the last time he'd given his life to his country one final time. Alex joined the Navy fresh out of high school. She fell in love with him while in high school, despite everyone saying she was too young and it would never last because he was a career military man.

The funny thing was, they didn't last—but her age had nothing to do with their ending.

Nope, the military took him from her... from his family, his friends, his life—over. As a member of Seal Team Six, Alex had been part of the elite. Jesse knew his job meant disappearing on dangerous missions for months, but she stood by him. Loving him from a distance and holding him close when he was home. Lord knew his last deployment hadn't been her first rodeo with being cut off.

And, as usual, Jesse didn't know the details. It wasn't permitted, and after all these years, she'd grown used to being in the dark. Being a military wife, that was how it had to be—secrecy and months on end of being a 'military widow.'

Except now, she *was* a widow.

The day the base general and chaplain pulled into her driveway, Jesse had been unloading the moving van. She and Alex had just bought the place, and he was due stateside in two weeks to help make it a home together.

Instead, he came home early in a pine box.

She remembered what she'd been doing when the two uniformed men walked up the porch steps. She'd been carrying a box of glasses into the kitchen. Jesse's brother, John, had been in the upstairs bedroom dropping off a box when the doorbell rang.

Like a scene from a horror movie, she turned, box in hand—to see two military personnel standing beyond the window of the front door. She'd always heard when a wife saw military officers at their door, there'd be no need for words. Their presence conveyed what their purpose was without speaking. But like a sick fascination with a car crash, you pass on the road, you just need to see it, or in her case, hear it anyway.

Jesse didn't remember the box slipping from her hands, but she would never forget the words from the Chaplain's mouth. He said that Alex's helicopter had been shot down while returning from a mission somewhere outside of Qatar. According to the official report, all members of the team were killed when an RPG struck the aircraft.

They recovered the wreckage and the members inside. They were later identified as the men of the Black Squadron—two pilots and two crew chiefs. There was nothing physical to identify Alex with, only his dog tags. Jesse absentmindedly reaches up and fingers the lone tag hanging from her neck.

The next few weeks were a blur. They held the funeral in town. Everyone came out to send the hometown hero off to Valhalla, his final resting place. The service was a haunting memory in her mind, and the folded American flag, paired with his dog tags on her nightstand, were the only proof she attended her husband's funeral.

Alex's mother lost her shit and had to be sedated the day of his service. His dad, bless his soul, stayed drunk as a skunk for days leading up to the funeral. Alex's younger brother, AJ, also in the Navy, was given leave for thirty days. They said he needed to be with his family as they repaired the hole from what Alex's death left behind.

AJ and Jesse had been close friends since high school. Their friendship started sophomore year, and from there, they'd been two peas in a pod. When Jesse's father died, AJ and she became inseparable. He'd become Jesse's rock through those tough times, strengthening their friendship into an unbreakable bond. Jesse knew AJ had a brother, but he'd been deployed with the Navy most of their sophomore year, and she hadn't met him until much later.

AJ always knew he wanted to follow in his brother's footsteps, and two weeks after high school graduation, he joined the Navy. Alex was one of the Navy's best intelligence officers—he'd made something of himself and had an honorable career at twenty-six.

Jesse's brother, John, was the local sheriff in their hometown of Campo. He joined the force when he turned twenty-one, not too long after earning his Criminal Justice degree at the University. John was three years older than her and married the woman who stole his heart, Allie. Allie was a schoolteacher like Jesse and worked at the same high school as her.

Jesse was surrounded by people who were military or law enforcement—so getting over Alex's death was harder—when everyone around her reminded her of him. They meant well. They checked on her daily, trying to get her to unpack or come out of the house. But Jesse didn't care. She didn't think she could stay in the house; that was like a living memory of the one thing she couldn't have. If it weren't for AJ or John, Jesse would've given up. She never expected to bury her partner in life so soon.

It was supposed to be their new beginning. Until buying this house, they'd lived on base in San Diego. But they'd decided it was time to try for kids, and with him being deployed so often, Jesse convinced him to move closer to family, and since Alex wanted that, too, they bought a house in Campo.

Campo was a small town in California where they'd grown up. It was only an hour's drive to the base in San Diego, and Alex decided he'd commute when he got stationed stateside. Campo is the home to the Pacific Southwest Railway Museum —but aside from that, it's small, with a population of about 2500 people.

The house they bought was two streets from his parents, and Jesse's brother lived two houses down from them. That seemed so trivial now. Staying in the house seemed like a betrayal to Alex. She couldn't fathom carrying on in the place they'd chosen together without him to make memories. As she looked around the mountain of memories, Jesse shook off her thoughts, deciding it was too hard to face them.

Striding up the stairs to the master bedroom, still packed in boxes, she closed the door behind her. The bed and nightstand were the only things set up. The nightstand held the flag and dog tags she'd been given at the funeral. She held them for the last couple of weeks as she cried to sleep.

She could still hear the whisper of his voice from the last time they talked. He'd told her he'd be home in two weeks—that was six weeks ago—when he was still alive.

Jesse couldn't remember what his touch felt like or what he smelled like. His memory was fading, piercing her heart with guilt that was suffocating. He'd been deployed for months. Hell, she couldn't even remember the last time he held her, or she'd kissed him—and now she couldn't do any of those things.

She undressed and slipped on one of his t-shirts. It was one of the few things she'd taken out of a box holding his belongings. His scent was still embedded in the fabric, though vanishing like her memories as more time passed. Jesse pulled the collar to her nose and inhaled... closing her eyes as a lone tear spilled down her cheek, staining it with the grief threatening to pull her under.

God, she missed him. He was half her soul. His love filled her heart, strengthening it, making it beat thunderously for everyone to hear. Now, with him gone, it was like a fragile glass jar—empty, missing the love that sustained the soul within her.

Chapter Two

ONE YEAR LATER....

The alarm sounded, waking Jesse from her blissful dreams—it was the realm she preferred, as she spent her nights with Alex there. Stretching, turning off the piercing beeping, she stood and went to the bathroom. Jesse returned to work teaching high school English. It's something to do to survive and keep her mind off him—her dead husband.

There were still unpacked boxes that held Alex's things, even after a year in the house. Jesse couldn't bring herself to touch them and wouldn't let anyone else near them. She'd emptied all the necessities to live there—her clothes and some photos. But beyond that, the walls were still bare, devoid of life. She couldn't hang reminders of what should have been.

"Morning, Jesse," AJ greeted her as he entered the kitchen. His parents agreed she shouldn't live alone. And since AJ was stationed at the base in San Diego, it made sense for him to move in. It took a lot of discussion and convincing on his part —but AJ moved in several months ago. It's good that he was there since he helped her with the house and kept Jesse from giving up on life.

"Morning, AJ, I gotta run. I have to be at the school in 15 minutes." She grabbed an apple and a bottle of water and headed out the door.

"Jesse, wait." AJ latched onto her arm. "Look, I want to know how you are—you don't leave your room when you're here. I'm worried about you."

"I'm fine... really. I can't face life beyond work right now." Pulling free of his grasp, she looked at him. The concern was etched in the lines of his face. He was still grieving, but his worry for her was clear.

"AJ, I know you're worried—Hell, you're grieving too. But I need time. Alex was my universe. I need to figure out how to live again... without him."

"I get it, Jesse. I miss him every day, too. I'm reminded that he isn't coming home every time I step on base. But he would want us to live... to move on. He wouldn't want you to wither away. I don't want you to become a shell of a person, Jess. You're family—my family."

His words cut her to the core—seeping into her empty heart like poison. "Thank you, AJ. You gave up your bachelor's life to be here for me; I'll always be grateful for that. I promise I'll get better. Just give me some time. You, being here... helps."

"Bachelor's life? Huh, that's funny, Jess. I'd trade it all to help you. I love you too...you know. Plus, it wasn't all it was cracked up to be—I can see why Alex loved being married to you. I'm not alone living here with you—EVEN if you stay holed up in your room all night." AJ winked at her as he pulled her into his arms and hugged her tight. The feeling of his lips against her head caused her to shiver. "Go on. I don't want to make you late. I just wanted you to know I'm here, so lean on me a little, ok? Oh, hey—I almost forgot. Mom and Dad are having dinner tonight—they want you to come. So, no excuses, you're going with me... be ready by six."

He disappeared out the front door and ran to his car.

Staring at where his car had been parked, Jesse couldn't help thinking about Alex. AJ was so much like him—if you didn't know them, you'd almost think they were twins. AJ was taller and leaner. He was muscular like Alex but not as bulky. Alex stayed in shape being a SEAL, so his workouts were rigorous.

AJ worked out every day and was a Ninjitsu Warrior. He was considered a Sigung instructor and trained other Naval Officers several days a week.

To say AJ was athletic was an understatement. It would be impossible for a woman or man not to take notice of his sculpted body. Jesse smiled at the thought. He was a blessing —Alex would be proud to know his brother had stepped up to care for her and protected her heart from being broken further.

Locking the door, She took the steps towards my car and looked around. This place was perfect for a family—the thought of it made her heart clench again. Glancing towards her brother's house, which sat diagonally to hers in the cul-de-sac, she saw Allie getting into her car. Working at the same school, Jesse knew she'd also be heading that way. As she passed by Allie's driveway, she tossed her hand in a half wave and honked at Jesse, making her sister-in-law laugh.

Waving back, Jesse shook her head in amusement as she walked to get the mail she'd forgotten about yesterday. Snatching the envelopes, she thumbed through the stack and climbed into her car. It was primarily bills, but a letter at the bottom caught her eye. It'd been postmarked recently, but what had her sucking in a breath was who the return address was from—Alex.

Tears filled her eyes as she fingered the return address—He'd been gone a year, so having a recent postmark seemed unusual. Flipping the envelope over, she noted a written message on the back.

> Dear Mrs. Holt,
> I found this letter in some of the equipment for SEAL Team Six. I don't mean to open your fresh wounds more, but I felt you may want it—it is addressed to you, after all. I couldn't bring myself to throw it away since it may be all you have left of him. He was a good man and is sorely missed by those who knew him. I hope this letter helps you find peace.
> Sincerely,
> Jack Wynn, Lt. Commander—US Navy

Her tears stained the envelope as she ran her finger along his words. Closing her eyes, she inhaled and folded the letter. She couldn't bring herself to open it. Tucking it inside her jacket pocket, she gripped the steering wheel. The weather was never cold. They didn't get an actual winter, but being October, mornings were in the fifties—today was no exception. With the chill of knowing what she held in her pocket, Jesse fought back a shiver.

She started the car and backed out, making her way towards work. School was her way of taking a break from the constant heartache. Working with a bunch of high school students left little room for wallowing in self-misery. Jesse stayed focused on them and ensured they met the success they were entitled to. And reading the letter now would lead her to hysterics—that wouldn't be fair to them.

"Morning, Mrs. Holt," several students hollered as Jesse entered the school's building, her mind still stuck on the note burning against her thigh.

Waving them off, she headed into her classroom. "Morning Guys, see you in English."

Jesse started teaching a year ago, just before Alex was killed. She'd been commuting from the base until they bought the house in Campo. Jesse's desk held framed pictures of her life with Alex—a life that didn't exist anymore. Everything, including her job, had become a painful reminder of her past.

She sat down and pulled the letter from her pocket, fingering the words written by Commander Wynn. It was like a message from the grave, a ghost whisper from Alex that was determined to haunt her still. She tucked the letter in her desk drawer, locking it for safekeeping. Resolving that she'd read once classes were done, Jesse put the letter out of sight, not out of mind. With it out of view, she wouldn't be tempted to read it during class.

Classes went by without cause. Before she knew it, the last bell was ringing. "See you later, Mrs. Holt," Katie, one of her best students, muttered, tossing her a wave as she left the room.

"See you tomorrow, Katie. Wonderful work on your essay analyzing 'The Great Gatsby.'"

Taking a deep breath, Jesse closed the classroom door behind Katie and returned to her desk. With uncertainty, she unlocked the drawer and pulled the message out. It was wrinkled like it'd been stuffed in a sweaty pocket and carried around for days—Alex probably wrote it out on a mission at some point. He did that often, then put it in the post when he got back to base. Jesse lifted the envelope to her nose, inhaling the smell of sweat, heat, and the imaginary scent of Alex on the paper. Sitting in her chair, she edged her finger under the seal. Careful not to rip the paper to keep it as perfect as possible, like embalming the dead before burial, she lifted the flap.

Resting the paper on her lap, Jesse closed her eyes. She prayed for composure before letting herself read over the words. She unfolded the pages with cautionary hands and lifted them to her eyes. The tears silently rolled down her face, staining the white linen paper with each drop that fell. The pages rested in her hands, turning her knuckles white as the blurry words began to make some sense. The letter felt like Alex was talking to her from the grave—tormenting her unintentionally. The panicked breaths grew faster, nearing a full-blown attack as Jesse scanned the last words Alex had penned.

My love,

In just a couple of weeks, we will be together again. I look forward to kissing your soft lips while making love to you. It feels like forever since I held you in my arms.

My Team and I are just hours away from the last mission. They say it should go smoothly, but this one holds more risk than the others, which is why I wrote to you. I had to tell you what you mean to me—your love has been my savior these last few months. The amount of death we've encountered has been tormenting.

The picture I keep of you tucked inside my vest reminds me of the beauty in this world. Starting a family with you is the only thing I long to do—and I can't wait to be home to start ours.

I love you wholeheartedly, but I need to say this. If something were to go wrong and I don't come home—I need to know you'll move on with your life. You are too beautiful and kind to wither away from loss. You deserve happiness and love. Remember this always in the event something goes bad over here. Jesse, know that I will do everything to come home to you. You are my world, and I will always love you.

Forever yours,

A.

Tears poured down her cheeks as she folded the letter. She placed it back in the envelope and shoved the tormented parchment into her jacket pocket again. It was as if Alex had a premonition before his mission and was preparing for the worst. He loved her. That was evident through his words—yet it didn't bring Jesse any closure. She could not see herself moving on anytime soon—even if it *was* his wish.

A soft rap on the door startled Jesse from her silent reverie. Glancing up, she noticed AJ standing on the other side of the door. Wiping the tears from her stained cheeks, Jesse walked over and waved him into the room.

He pushed past her. "Jesse, what the *hell?* You weren't home when I got there. I freaked out... Allie said you were still here and thought you were working late. But from the looks of it— working is not what you've been doing." He pulled Jesse into the safety of his arms, drawing out a full-on sob. "Jess, what happened?" leaning her away from his hold, AJ brushed a loose strand of hair from her eyes. "Come here, sit down, and talk to me. Did someone hurt you?"

Leading Jesse to her desk, he eased her into her chair and leaned against her desk. Jesse couldn't speak. It was just too hard to find the words she needed to say. Instead, she removed the letter from her jacket. Shoving it into his hands, she closed her eyes and hiccupped a sob. "It's a letter... from Alex."

His eyes widened as her words registered. Jesse watched as he scanned the message. With red-rimmed eyes, he finally looked up. "Jesus, Jess. Where did you get this?"

"It was in the mailbox this morning. I didn't read it until just before you got here." Pushing herself up from the chair, she tugged it from his hands. "We should go. Your parents will be waiting for us."

As she started to gather her things, AJ grabbed her arm. "Jesse, this is major. You should have called me—I was worried sick about you, and now I see I was right to be."

"God... Alex loved you. More than life itself. But he's right, Jess. You deserve to find happiness again."

Snatching free from his grasp, Jesse stormed past him. "It's so easy for you to say that. *You* weren't married to him. *You* weren't planning on starting a family. *You* weren't planning on growing old together. Sure, you're his brother. You loved him. *But I need him like air.* So, don't *tell* me what I deserve. I *deserve* to have my husband here—with me. *Not dead.* I have every right to deal with him being gone however I want."

"JESSE." AJ's voice cracks as he pulls her into his arms. Placing a soft kiss on her head, he sighs. "Man... I'm sorry. I didn't mean it like that. I'm just saying you're a beautiful woman, and I knew Alex. He wouldn't want you sad forever. You're right. You need time to mourn—he's only been gone a year."

I'M SORRY, AJ... I—I get so mad when I think about what should've been. But you're right. Alex would be angry knowing I live just existing every day—it's just hard. I am deeply thankful for your presence and support during this difficult time, and I should not vent my frustrations on you. Come on, let's go. Your parents will be pissed if we're late."

AJ's jeep was parked halfway on the sidewalk. Cocking her head, "Um, AJ?"

Waving his hands in the air, he lets out a little chuckle. "What? I was freaked out. I thought something had happened to you. I mean, Christ, it's almost six o'clock. You're the only one here."

Looking into the parking lot, Jesse realized she was the only car in the lot aside from his. "I lost track of time. Sorry."

Jesse watched AJ climb into his truck, his muscular arms flexing as he hoisted himself into the driver's seat. She was lucky to have him in her life. He'd given up so much to be her rock and help her navigate her new normal—of course, he'd never admit such.

Being single and living with a single woman he wasn't dating dampened a guy's romantic life. But AJ never let it bother him, or he kept that lifestyle out of sight. Jesse felt an over-whelming sense of thankfulness towards him for his significant role in her healing process.

Her drive home in silence led to a thousand thoughts plaguing her mind. Alex would be furious that she was sinking into depression. He would want her to live again at some point... heck, part of her would like the same for him if the roles were reversed. But the thought of a life without him made her stomach revolt at the thought of him with someone else. Pushing those thoughts away, she focused on the here and now.

After parking in the driveway, Jesse locked her car door and jumped into the passenger seat of AJ's jeep. He'd followed her home so they could take one car to his parents.

Casting a sideways glance at him as he drove, Jesse smiled. "Your parents are pissed."

"Nah, I called them when you weren't home and told them you had to stay a little longer at work, so we'd obviously be late. They knew I wouldn't let you drive alone and would bring you over."

Laughing out loud at his earnest expression when he spoke, Jesse smacked his arm. "Right, because two streets are too far for a girl to travel alone. AJ, seriously, what would I do without you?"

AJ was a girl's dream catch. The woman who snagged his heart would be lucky to be loved by him. Thinking about how much she must dampen his dating life, Jesse took a breath and squeezed his arm. "AJ, are you sure living with me is right for you? I mean, look at you. Surely you want to find a woman to go home to?"

Flexing his muscles beneath her hold, he leaned over and kissed his bicep. "What—you think these arms make me sexy?" Jesse rolled her eyes. "Seriously Jess... I already have a woman to come home to. Why would I need someone else?"

They pulled into his parent's driveway and parked. "AJ, be serious. You're a good-looking guy. I don't want to stifle your need for romance."

Waggling his eyebrows, "Jess, I do not need romance... besides, I'm holding out for the girl of my dreams to fall in love with me. She just needs time."

AJ darted from the jeep towards his parent's front door. Sitting for a moment longer, Jesse let his words mull around in her head. His words felt cryptic, but she shook it off. Sometimes AJ talked nonsense—but for the first time, she felt like there might be someone he was into... she just hoped she wasn't ruining his chances at a future with her.

Inhaling the fresh air, Jesse mustered up the courage and exited the jeep. The experience of being with Alex's parents had its ups and downs. She usually cried first, then ended the evening laughing at old stories of childhood antics.

Looking at the house, Jesse knew starting a life with someone else would never happen. These people were her family, and starting over with someone else felt like a betrayal to them. She couldn't fathom being with an outsider. This place and these people were her home.

Chapter Three

DINNER WAS tame for the first time in months. Jesse was relieved his parents didn't question why she'd been at work so late. They knew she threw herself into her job to avoid falling into depression even more than she already struggled with. As they ate, Jesse noticed AJ staring at her off and on throughout the meal.

Perturbed that he was looking at her like she might crack any moment, Jesse snapped. "AJ, why are you watching me like that?"

Shrugging his shoulders, "I wasn't looking at you... Jess, I am just worried about you is all."

His parents exchanged a glance, confusion in their eyes. Betty, Alex, and AJ's mother looked at her with concern. "Jesse, are you ok? You look like you haven't been sleeping well, honey."

"I'm fine. Honestly, I am. Betty, please don't worry about me. AJ has been helpful. I wouldn't be able to function without him," smiling at Betty, Jesse cut her eyes towards AJ.

"OK, well, let us know if you need anything... Please, we're here for you. We know it's hard. I miss him every day, too—but having you around helps with the pain." His mother's eyes welled up as she gathered the dishes from the table.

"I'll just take these into the kitchen." She gathered the dishes. "Anyone want dessert?"

The room became suffocating, and she stood. The urge to flee was overwhelming. Betty's emotions were taking a toll on Jesse after her earlier shock at Alex's letter. "Actually, I need to get home. I have some papers I need to grade—and I'm tired for once."

It wasn't a complete lie. She did have papers to grade. Sleep, however, wasn't something she would have. It hadn't been for the last twelve months, so tonight likely wouldn't be any different.

"AJ, you mind running me home?"

He stood and tipped his head toward his mom as they approached the door. "Nah, I'm ready too. Mom and Dad, thanks for dinner. We gotta bolt."

"AJ, do you mind waiting for a second? I want to talk to you alone for a minute." His father met them at the front door.

Handing Jesse the keys, AJ turned toward his dad. "Ah, yeah, sure. Here, Jess, take the keys. I'll be out in a minute."

Hugging him quickly, Jesse pressed a kiss on his cheek. "Thanks, Dad. You guys mean the world to me."

"You take care of yourself, Jesse. Alex wouldn't want you unwell."

She stepped outside, and AJ shut the door behind her. She'd only been sitting alone for a few moments when AJ hopped in the driver's seat. "Everything ok?"

"Yeah, Dad, just reminding me of my role in life."

"What does that mean? Role in life…?"

"Nothing—don't worry about it. He's just worried about everything going on with you."

"Everything going on. Whatever, I'm too tired to care, anyway. Your parents mean well, but it's hard, ya know?"

Turning to look at him, Jesse was surprised to find his eyes on her. "What?"

Shaking his head, he pressed his lips together and pulled the car out of the driveway. The ride was silent, neither of them saying a word. As they pulled into the driveway and parked, AJ turned and sighed. His eyes held my gaze for a moment, then he spoke.

"Jess, I know that letter tore you up. But listen to me when I say this—Alex would never want you in this much pain. If there is one thing I know about my brother, it's how much he loved you. He would want you to live again. You have the right to mourn, but I won't sit back and watch you wither away. I care about you too much. Jess, I love you too. Do you understand?"

Jesse couldn't say anything as she stared at him—he was right, but she still wasn't ready to hear it.

"AJ, I love you too and am so grateful for everything you do… But I am not ready to move on—I don't know if I ever will be."

He reached up, cupping her cheek. The pad of his thumb brushed over her skin as his words came out in a whisper.

"Jess, don't let sadness blind you to something that could be right in front of your face."

His hand pulled away, and he climbed out of the Jeep. Jesse watched him as he walked to the house, his sadness visible through his slumped shoulders. Sitting in the Jeep alone, she listened to the sounds of the night. Her heart and head were not on talking terms anymore. One wanted her to move on. The other was stuck in an unforgiving past.

Unable to move from her spot, she just sat—waiting. There was no way she could see herself in love again. Her heart was just too broken. Pushing from the confines of the jeep, Jesse took each step to the front door, one at a time. When she entered the foyer, AJ had already locked himself away in his room. Walking past his door, she paused—placing her palm on the closed door; she listened.

His gentle sobs echoed through the wood, reminding her that his pain was no less than hers. Resting my head on the door frame, she sent a silent prayer to God—begging him to release them all from this hell. Neither of them deserved to feel the loss. They were both hurting... equally, and she needed to remember that. She was open about her heartache, but AJ kept his hidden behind closed doors.

Turning from his door, Jesse found herself in her room. Staring at the painful reminder on her nightstand, she collapsed on the bed. The tears took over, and Jesse lay there crying until exhaustion claimed her.

THE BLARING of her alarm woke her with a startle. Stretching, Jesse realized she'd fallen asleep in yesterday's clothes. Scrambling from the bed, Jesse bolted to the bathroom. Usually showering at night, she would have enough time to get ready and make it to work on time. Rushing as her life depended on it, Jesse quickly showered and dressed. Running into the kitchen, she wasn't surprised AJ had already left. She smiled when she saw the note on the counter.

Jess—won't be home tonight. Something's come up at work, and I am needed there. Leftovers are in the fridge... please don't stay in your room. Eat. I'll be back tomorrow night. Maybe we can grab some dinner! See you later. Love, AJ.

Warmth spread throughout her body, reading his words. AJ cared about and worried about her, even when he wasn't here. Snatching an apple and water, Jesse bolted out the door. Allie had already left, which meant she was late. Hurrying to her car, she cranked it and shoved it into gear. Being late was not something she liked—at all. She was relieved when she pulled into the school parking lot with ten minutes to spare. Today was going to feel rushed, no matter what.

She spotted Allie as soon as she stepped into her hallway. She was talking to a couple of their friends and co-workers. Jesse uses the word friends loosely. It was a group of girls she'd had gone to high school with, who'd all returned after college. They'd gone their separate ways for college but somehow ended up together. Jesse had distanced herself from almost everyone after the funeral, but they never gave up trying to break down her walls.

"Hey, Jess!" Carmen was the school's cheerleading coach and was always trying to get Jesse to help her out.

Jesse forced a smile and paused. "What's up, Carmen... I'm running late. Overslept this morning."

She smiled at Jesse as she followed her toward her classroom. "Look, I know you'll probably say no... but—Allie and I are going out tomorrow. We want you to come. You need a night out and tomorrow's Friday, so we won't have to be at work the next day. What do ya say?" She stuck her lip out like she was pouting—trying to coax Jesse into going.

"I don't know. I'm just not ready."

"Just think about it. A girl's night out is just what you need. I'm not saying pick anyone up... just dinner, drinks, and dancing."

Jesse rubbed across the bridge of her nose. She had no doubt her expression made her look like she was in pain. "Ah, I'll think about it, ok?"

She squealed like a teenager. "Great! Allie will be so happy! We can ride together. That way, you can drink your sorrows..." Jesse's face must have fallen because she winced and immediately recanted her words. "Shit, Jess... me and my big mouth. I mean, you can drink and not worry about picking up a guy. You deserve that." Pulling her into a hug, she whispered, "I know you miss him."

Jesse pulled out of her embrace, fighting back the tears, "I gotta go. I'll let you know tomorrow, ok?"

Spinning on her feet, Jesse hurried away from Carmen towards my room. She wiped the lone tear that threatened to fall as she pushed inside her classroom. She hurried to her desk and sat down. There were several students already seated and waiting for the day to start.

"Mrs. Holt, are you ok?" Glancing up, Jesse found Katie standing in front of her desk.

"Um, yeah. Why?"

She shifted on her feet like she was uneasy. "I heard you and Ms. Kirkpatrick in the hall. I know she upset you... I just wanted to make sure you were ok."

Katie was Jesse's best student—she had a promising future ahead of her if she kept up the hard work she did. "Thanks, Katie. I'm fine—it just gets me now and again." Jesse bobbed her head, trying to convince Katie and herself that she was okay.

"Yeah, I understand. But she's right, you know. You deserve a night out. It's ok to feel sad—but you're too pretty a woman to stay holed up in your house all the time."

Blushing at her words, Jesse smiled. "Katie, that's sweet of you to say. But I don't always stay holed up in my house."

"All due respect, Mrs. Holt... You do. I live just a few houses over—and I can honestly say if it weren't for that hunk you had living with you... well, you'd turn into a cat lady. Give yourself a break. Go out and have some fun. I'm sure your late husband would want that for you."

She was wise for her years and probably correct, even if hearing her say the words was hard. "You're right, Katie. He wouldn't want me to stop living. Thank you—you're wise for such a young lady."

Standing, Jesse pulled her into a quick hug before shooing her to her desk. Once she was seated, the class went by quickly. The students Jesse taught were great. They were all involved and worked hard at everything they did. She was thankful for them and worked just as hard to ensure they did well.

Once class was done, Jesse went into the hall, searching for Carmen. She was standing in the student bathrooms, giving several students a lecture. They had been screwing off in the bathroom, and she was pissed.

Clearing her throat, "Ms. Kirkpatrick, you got a second?"

Cutting her off mid-rant, she spun to say something. She thought Jesse was another student interrupting her moment. "Mrs. Holt... I thought you were a student." Turning back to the kids, "Go on, get to class. And never let me see you doing that crap again. Got it?" The kids nodded, taking off down the hall.

"Damn kids—they were freaking rolling the bathroom, or at least were going to if I hadn't come in here to wash my hands."

Laughing, she looked up at Jesse. "What's up?"

"Well, a smart student of mine talked some sense into me. I'll go with you tomorrow."

Carmen jumped into the air. "Yes! Oh, sorry. I am just damn happy you're going to leave your cats and come out with us. I'll tell Allie, she's going to flip!!"

"Wait—I don't have cats..."

She hurried off down the hall. "Maybe not yet, but you're on your way!"

She giggled as she ducked into her classroom. Damn, maybe she was turning into a hermit. Jesse just felt guilty for living when Alex was gone. Hurrying back to class, she sighed—regretting her decision already. Maybe she'd cancel tomorrow. Jesse didn't know if she had the strength to endure a girl's night.

Chapter Four

WALKING INTO THE HOUSE, silence greeted her. Remembering AJ was gone until the next day, Jesse's heart pounded against her ribs. It was the first time in a long time she'd been alone in the house overnight since burying Alex. Taking one step at a time, her legs carried her into the kitchen. Opening the fridge, she found a container with a handwritten note saying, 'Eat me' on the top shelf. The corners of her lips edged into a smile as she slipped it out, removing the lid to heat it.

AJ was taking care of her as usual. Alex would be so proud of him. He'd turned into such a fantastic man, and here she was hogging his time—part of her felt guilty, but the other part couldn't bear the thought of not having AJ around. Selfish, she knew—but she needed him more and more every day. She pulled a bottle of wine from the fridge door as the food heated in the microwave. A glass would hopefully help her sleep, and being in this empty house—she needed to eat and pass out.

Jumping to the sound of her phone, she nearly spilled the glass she'd been holding. Fumbling through her bag discarded on the counter, she slipped out her cell phone. AJ's face lit up the screen, making her smile. Glancing at the time, she figured he must also be getting ready to eat dinner.

"Hey, AJ. What's up?" glancing around, she grabbed the wine and filled her glass with more.

"Jess, I wanted to call and make sure you were ok. It's the first time I've left you alone overnight."

"AJ, I'm a grown woman. The boogeyman won't come for me." chuckling, she swigged the sweet liquid, the cool bitterness flowing down her throat.

"Glad you have a sense of humor—it's nice to hear. Seriously though. I was worried. I didn't like leaving you alone."

She could hear the guys hollering at AJ in the background, "AJ, it sounds like you have some hungry sailors. Go and eat with the guys. Lord knows I monopolize your time enough. I'm fine—really. I'm just going to eat, drink my wine... maybe take a bath, and then go to bed."

"OK—if you're sure. I'll be home tomorrow night. We can grab dinner when I get back."

"Oh, I almost forgot—I'm going out with Carmen and Allie. Just drinks and dinner."

His silence at the other end had her doubting her decision to go out. Maybe it was too soon. "Did you hear me?"

"Yeah, sorry, the guys are being asshats. Hey, I'm glad you're going out. You need to. I'll see you when you get home then. Be careful. If you need anything, call me... Jess, I know I tell you this often, but I care about you."

"I know AJ—I care about you, too. I love you... I couldn't do this without you. Now go eat with your friends!"

She smiled as they disconnected the call and placed the phone in her pocket. Grabbing her food and more wine, Jesse headed upstairs. She sat on her bed, wolfing down the leftover food from AJ's mom. Man, she could cook—Jesse was full and starting to feel like she was on the edge of a food coma. Pushing off the bed, Jesse headed into the bathroom. Still holding the remnants of her half-drunk wine, Jesse elected to take a bath. Maybe the warm water and wine would help her into dreamland.

Turning on the water, Jesse stood and stripped herself bare. Taking in her reflection, Jesse cringed at how thin she'd gotten... the depression was taking a toll on more than just her head. It was starting to affect her body. Huffing, she slipped her feet into the bubbly water and slid down. Resting against the edge, she closed her eyes. The water felt divine as her body sunk into the tub. The heat of the liquid relaxed her almost immediately.

Feeling so content, she couldn't help but let her mind drift to Alex. Jesse missed him so much it hurt—closing her eyes, she could almost see him standing there. They were together again in her head, and she was being held in his embrace. A tear slipped from her eye, tracing its way down her cheek and into the warm water. Giving in to the darkness, Jesse drifted off to sleep.

She woke several hours later, shivering, still in the bathtub. The water was now frigid. Her body began to shake. Releasing the drain, Jesse got up and wrapped a towel around herself. Quickly drying off, she threw on a T-shirt and headed into the bedroom. Noting it was twelve-thirty, Jesse realized she'd slept in the water for nearly four hours.

Tugging down the worn t-shirt that had belonged to Alex, Jesse crawled under the covers. Wrapping her arms around the extra pillows like they were another person, Jesse buried her face in the silky sheets. Trying not to tear up, she prayed for the pain to go away. She missed Alex, but the heartache was killing her slowly.

Chapter Five

THE ALARM JOLTED Jesse from her slumber. Grunting, Jesse stretched and placed her feet on the floor. It was Friday—which meant a night out with the girls from work. Unsure if she wanted to go, she considered canceling them. Carmen would understand, and she was certain Allie wouldn't judge her. She thought about what her excuse would be.

After getting dressed, I walked downstairs. As I walked into the kitchen, I walked straight into a body.

"What the *fuck?*" I screamed, nearly falling on my ass.

"Whoa... Jess—It's me. Calm down."

Her brother grabbed her arms to steady her. "Damn, sorry—I let myself in. I was worried about you. You didn't answer your cell when I called this morning."

The realization dawned on Jesse. She'd left her phone in her pants pocket last night, which meant it was dead as a doornail. "Shit, I forgot to charge the damn thing."

Turning, she quickly hustled up the stairs, finding her pants discarded on the bathroom floor. Sure enough, inside the pocket was her dead phone. She hurried back down the steps. "Yep," waving it in the air, "It's dead."

She strolled back into the kitchen. "You could have called out —or better yet, rang the doorbell." Quirking her eyebrow at him.

"Why the hell would I do that? You gave me a key—remember? Geez... give a guy a break. I was worried about you. I know AJ isn't here, and it's the first time you've been in this house alone overnight. What can I say? I'm an overprotective brother," he winked at her, smirking.

Wrapping her arms around him, Jesse hugs him. "I know— and thank you. I'm just giving you a hard time. I love you for being overprotective."

And that was the truth. She couldn't have asked for a better brother. Plus, having him next door was a bonus. As she released her hold, his words hit her. "Wait, a minute. How did you know AJ was gone?" Her eyes probed him, waiting for an answer.

"Well, for one—he called me and told me. And two, his Jeep isn't here. It doesn't take Einstein to figure out he didn't come home."

Flipping him off, "Bite me. Whatever. I got to get to school. I hate being late." She walked out the front door, John following close behind.

"Allie said you're going out with them tonight."

His stare made Jesse uncomfortable. "Yeah—you have a problem with that?"

"Jess, I am glad you're finally getting out of the house. And being with your friends will be good for you. You need to get back out there and live. It's been a year... It's time." He brushed his hand across her arm. "It's what Alex would want."

Everyone knew what Alex wanted, but none knew what she wanted. Jesse wanted him... *alive*. "*Stop*. Please. Everyone keeps telling me that. It doesn't help. I'm going because I don't want to be a cat lady. Not for anything else."

"A cat lady?" his laugh caused her to snort at the ridiculousness of her words. "You could never be a cat lady—I wouldn't let you. Don't you hate cats, anyway?"

They both erupted into laughter, unable to hold back their laughter. "Yeah, I hate them. You're right—no way I'm turning into a cat lady. But still... I'm going tonight for dinner and friends. That's going to be hard enough. My heart can't handle real living. That will be a long time from now—at least, I think it will. It doesn't matter, anyway. I have AJ."

John gave her a speculative look but kept his comment to himself. Instead, he nodded his head as she got into her car. "Yeah, AJ. He cares about you, but getting out will be good for you. It's a start, Jess. That's all we can ask of you. Baby steps, sis, baby steps."

John turned and jogged to his house. He disappeared through his front door before she could say anything. Instead, she threw the car in reverse and backed out of the driveway. There was no telling what Carmen had planned for tonight—but Jesse decided she'd tough it out. Maybe everyone would leave her alone and stop trying to push her into something she wasn't ready for. She wanted more time in her wallowing. It was something she needed.

Carmen was waiting for her when she pulled into the school. "Hey, Jess! Are you ready for tonight? You're not gonna ditch us, are you?" Her head cocked to the side as she watched Jesse, waiting for a response.

"Nah, I'll be there. Where are we going exactly?"

"We're headed into San Diego. We want to try a new club there, and my friend is the bouncer. Allie will be the DD tonight, so we can all ride together. We will meet up at your house so you can't back out... Sound good? Oh, and you best dress hot. I know you're going for the company—but I can't have you stifling my man-whoring ways. And if you look like the cat lady, it will fuck my chances of finding Mr. Right."

Damn, Carmen hadn't changed a bit since high school. "Yeah, whatever. I'll dress nicely. What time?"

Carmen walked away, turning her head slightly. "Six. Be ready. We have an hour ride, and I don't want to get out there too late."

"Yeah, I'll be ready."

What had she gotten herself into? She was half tempted to tell her never mind, but seeing Katie walk by and wave reminded Jesse that even the students thought she would turn into a cat lady. Inwardly groaning, Jesse walked into the school. She might dread tonight but would fake it as best she could.

The day seemed to drag on, but she was finally home and standing in the middle of her closet. She had nothing to wear. Shooting a quick text to Allie to tell her she wasn't going because her wardrobe sucked, Jesse threw herself onto the bed and buried her head under the pillow.

"Oh, *hell* no. Get up." Peering out from under the pillow, she found Allie and Carmen standing at her bedroom door.

"Woman, you should lock your door. But it doesn't matter—get up. You're getting dressed right now."

Tossing the pillow at Carmen, "I don't have anything to wear. I'm not going."

"Jess, I brought you a dress. *You. Are. Going.*" Carmen flung a blue piece of fabric at me.

Catching it in mid-air, "You can't be serious? Where is the dress?" Jesse shook her head and pushed the tiny scrap of fabric down on the bed beside her.

"Get up and put that damn dress on, or I will do it for you."

"You wouldn't dare..." Jesse held her stare, realizing that she would force it on her.

Carmen started towards Jesse. Her hands balled into fists as Allie watched from the door, offering no help. "Wait!" snatching the dress, she ran towards the bathroom. "I'll put the damn thing on."

Calling this tiny piece of fabric a dress was a laugh riot. It was tight, showing off all Jesse's curves, and stopped just above her knees. Its sleeves, or lack thereof, were two strips of fabric that crisscrossed at the back. The back was open down to the top of her butt cheeks, leaving very little to the imagination.

Stepping out of the bathroom, "I cannot wear this. Look at me!"

Rubbing her palms down the front of her thighs, Jesse looked up to find them standing with their mouths agape.

"What?? See, I told you I look like a hooker."

Allie was the first to speak. "No, girl—you look amazing!"

"You have to wear that. The color brings out your eyes. Please, Jess... wear it for me?" Carmen batted her eyes at Jesse. "You'll help me score tonight. I promise to keep the guys away from you—but you can't take that off. You look gorgeous."

Pulling at the hem with her fingers, "Fine, but I swear if one person calls me a hooker, you're bringing me home. Got it?"

"Jess, if someone calls you a hooker, I'll deck them. You're the farthest thing from a hooker."

Smiling, Jesse grabbed some lip gloss and headed out the door behind them. Her phone chirped as they entered the kitchen. Unlocking the screen, Jesse saw a text from AJ. He was staying out in San Diego for drinks with the guys since she was going out. Happy he was finally doing something other than babysitting me, Jesse smiled.

"What are you smiling about over there?" Carmen tried to see who had texted her.

"Stop! It was just AJ. He's hanging out with the guys on base. I'm glad he's getting out. I feel like I am dampening his action with girls. Maybe he'll get lucky."

As the words left her mouth, Jesse got a sickening feeling in the pit of her stomach. She shook her head and pushed the thought of him with another woman away. She had no right to be jealous—but oddly enough, part of her was.

"Right, I'm sure you want him to get lucky." Carmen chuckled to herself.

"What do you mean by that?" cocking her eyebrow, she stared at her friend.

"You know, we always thought you and AJ would get together. You two were inseparable in school. And since he's living here now... I figure you'll fall in love with him again."

"What? No. He lives here to help. Seriously—Alex was his brother. Us together? That would be wrong."

"Would it, though?"

Jesse stood, contemplating her words. Her jealousy when thinking of him with others made her question her loyalty to Alex. But Carmen was right. She *had* loved AJ first..., and then she met Alex.

Allie snapped them from the awkward silence, "Alright, let's get this show on the road."

"Are you coming, Jess?"

Nodding, she made a beeline for the car. She hadn't slipped inside when someone let out a loud wolf whistle. "Damn— who are you and what have you done with my sister?" Looking up, she saw John standing next to Allie. "Jess, you look fantastic! Maybe I should tag along. You'll need me to beat off guys with a stick."

Allie wrapped her arms around his neck, planting a long, sensual kiss on his lips, "Stop it, baby. Leave Jess alone. We just got her to agree to leave the house. You're going to undo all our hard work."

He kissed her back, pulling her against his enormous frame harder. "Baby, you look good, too. Maybe I should keep you here for myself."

"Ewwww, standing right here, guys. Allie, can you get in the car, please? We are ready to go." Jesse made a gagging sound as he released Allie and shot her a knowing grin.

"Jess, be careful, ok? Y'all need anything—call me. I'll be there in a flash."

"Alright. Love you, honey," Allie called out as she got behind the steering wheel. "You bitches ready to go?"

"Yes, already. Hurry before Jess jumps out of the car." Carmen laughed as Allie backed them out of the driveway. San Diego was an hour's drive. Resting her head against the cool glass of the car's window, Jesse must have dozed off because she was woken by someone jabbing her fingers into her ribs.

"Wake up, sleeping beauty, we're here!"

Her eyes fluttered open, and she slowly took the sight of the busy city out the car window. The sun had set, but the lights had the entire block illuminated. "Alright. The club is right there," Carmen pointed to a building that had people lined up around the corner, "like I said, my friend is the bouncer, so he will get us in ahead of everyone. Jess, you ready for this?"

"Nope—but too late now. Let's get this over with, shall we?"

Stepping from the car's safety, Allie and Carmen grabbed an elbow, dragging her towards the club entrance. "Let's go."

The three made their way across the busy street towards the entrance. Jesse's stomach was doing flip-flops as she thought about Alex. While she knew it wasn't, she couldn't shake the feeling this was wrong. It was too late to back out, so she'd have to put on a fake smile and be a big girl.

Chapter Six

THE LINE TO get into the club was wrapped around the corner to the backside of the building. Carmen dragged them to the front of the line, bypassing a horde of people. "Excuse me... coming through."

The groans and stares from the folks standing in the front of the line were less than friendly. "Hey, Mac," Carmen called out to a burly-looking guy at the door.

"Carmen. You made it—and you brought some friends." He looked Jesse and Allie over, his eyes roaming a little longer on Jesse than she liked.

"Yeah. This is Jesse and Allie. We work together." Carmen pulled him in for a hug.

Several of the girls in line behind us started making a fuss about her breaking in line, "Hey fuck off—you'd be jumping at the chance to get VIP treatment." Carmen shot them a bird as Mac ushered them through the doors.

"Damn Carmen, if teachers looked like your friend here when I was in school, I might have paid attention."

Jesse's cheeks blushed from his words, causing her to pull at the hem of her dress. Everything about standing there had her feeling uncomfortable in her skin.

Carmen must've noticed her reaction because she swatted his arm as they moved through the crowded entry. "Mac—knock it off... we had a hard enough time getting her to come out. The last thing I need is you fucking it up before she ever gets inside."

"Yeah, yeah. Even so, she's a looker."

Smiling, Jesse pushed her way past him, rolling her eyes as she shook her head at Carmen. "I told you I shouldn't have worn this damn dress. Everyone's staring at me."

Jesse wanted to crawl under a table and hide. This was precisely the attention she didn't want. Allie put her hand on her arm. "Jess, please—you look hot. Enjoy the looks. It doesn't mean anything... unless you want it to. You're in control here, not them."

She was nodding her head even though her gut churned with unease. Jesse continued moving through the crowd. Carmen pointed towards an empty table. "Let's sit down and get some drinks!"

The crowd was lively, and as they sat down, Jesse took the chance to take in the atmosphere. People seemed to be enjoying themselves. The vibe of the place was friendly but fun.

"I want a drink," Carmen hollered over the loud music. "Jess, go with me to the bar."

"Take Allie. I just want to people-watch. Please get me a Mojito—I need something to calm my nerves."

Carmen cocked her hip and stuck her lip out, pouting, "Fine, but next time you're coming with me."

She and Allie turned, heading towards the bar. Jesse couldn't help but giggle at them, even though she felt far from excited. They meant well, and she was grateful for having them as friends—but this was still a hard step for her. She knew her friends wouldn't let her sink into the darkness threatening her daily.

"Is this seat taken?"

Meeting the eyes of the masculine voice speaking to her, Jesse was taken aback to find a handsome guy staring at her. "I'm sorry?" Panic set in as he moved to the empty seat across from her. Her eyes scanned the crowd, willing Carmen or Allie back.

"I asked if this seat was taken. My buddies and I saw you and your friends. We wanted to see if we could join you."

He was gorgeous with a breathtaking smile, but it wasn't Alex or AJ. Jesse opened her mouth to tell them she wasn't interested but was cut off by Carmen's voice. "Nope, it's not taken —please join us."

Carmen sashayed around Jesse, taking his hand in hers. "I'm Carmen. That's Jesse and Allie. You are?"

"Wyatt." He kissed her hand as he brought her knuckles to his lips. "And those two bozos," ticking his head towards the two guys walking their way. "Are Bryan and Alex."

Jumping to her feet, Jesse bolted toward the bar, nearly tripping over the table as she did. "Excuse me."

"Shit." Jesse heard Allie mutter behind her, pushing through the crowd to catch up to her hurried escape. "Jess—wait a second."

Coming to a stop at the bar, Jesse flagged the bartender down, "A shot of something strong, please."

She needed something to dampen the pain boiling to the surface, threatening to spill out right there in the open.

"Jess." Allie pressed her hand on Jesse's shoulder. "Jess, come on—look at me."

"Just leave me, Allie. I knew this was a mistake—I should have stayed home. I'm not ready."

Jesse slammed back the shot of tequila almost as quickly as the bartender sat it down in front of her. The liquid burned as it slid down Jesse's throat, causing her to inhale sharply.

"Jess, you can't just hide away forever. Would you react that way if you have a student named Alex? Please, he wouldn't want you like this."

Jesse turned, glaring at Allie. "You don't get it. He was my *entire* world, Allie. And now—well, he's dead."

Turning back around, Jesse caught the bartender's eyes and motioned for another drink. "Bring me another. Allie," Jesse cut her eyes toward her sister-in-law. "Go back and have fun. I'm not ruining your night, but here is where I'll sit—drinking my heart away... Ok?"

Allie stood frozen, unsure of what to do. Jesse could sense the sadness and worry pouring off her like a beacon. "Jess. Seriously?"

Jesse arched a brow as Allie cocked her head, hand on her hip. "Dead serious. Just go—leave me alone, please."

Tipping another shot back, Jesse's goal suddenly became getting drunk enough not to care about life.

"Fine, but I will be watching from our seats—Jesse, you can't sit here all night, but I'll leave you alone for a little bit."

Jesse saw her walk off from the corner of her eye, but not before whispering something to the bartender at the other end. He came back to where she was sitting and smiled. "Doll, you look like you could use an ear. You alright?"

His smile seemed genuine as he spoke, making Jesse comfortable. He appeared to be an older gentleman, maybe in his late fifties. "I just don't want to be here. But my friends," motioning to the seats Allie and Carmen were sitting in, "thought I needed a night out. They were afraid I was turning into a cat lady."

Laughing, "You don't strike me as a cat person. Why would they think that?"

The warmth of his eyes made her feel like he was a dad talking to his daughter, and even though he was a stranger, Jesse started talking. "What makes you think I'm not a cat person?" She smirked, holding his gaze.

"I don't know… you look like more of a dog person. I'm Mike, by the way." Holding his hand out for her to shake.

Gripping it firmly, "Jesse. Nice to meet you, Mike. So, I'm just going to sit here and drink my misery away. Any recommendations on what poison I should use?"

"Well, you're far too pretty to drink yourself silly, but I'd say stick with tequila. It'll do the trick for ya. How about I whip you up a tequila sunrise?"

"Sounds good. Start a tab—I ain't moving from this spot until they are ready to leave."

"Well, can't say I understand why—but you're safe here, Jesse. I won't let anyone bother you."

"Thanks, Mike, you're a nice bartender."

Jesse lost count of how many drinks she'd had, but she'd been sitting at the bar for over an hour. Carmen and Allie had come over to check on her a few times, but Jesse dismissed them—telling them to leave her be until they were ready. The alcohol was starting to hit her, and she stood. A wave of dizziness hit her, and Jesse reached out, steadying herself on the bar.

"Mike, can you point the bathroom out to me—I think I need to take a minute."

Frowning slightly, he pointed towards the back of the club. "It's that way. You sure you're ok?"

Waving him off, "Yeah, save my seat, will ya?"

Turning, Jesse headed away from the bar. Her legs felt unsteady, matching the aching beat of her heart. It was apparent the alcohol was messing with her senses. Stumbling, she fell into someone coming out of the back hallway that led to the bathrooms.

"Whoa there, sexy—you looking for someone?"

The guy was huge, taking up most of the hallway, but Jesse tried to shake him off. "Umm, no—the bathroom actually, excuse me."

Jesse tried pushing past him, but he grabbed her arm. Why are you running off so fast? Let's get to know each other. You look mighty fine in that dress. It's a shame you don't have someone with you. I saw you all by yourself at the bar earlier—let's change that."

"I said, excuse me. I'm not interested." Yanking her arm from his fingers, she stumbled back slightly.

"Awe come on—don't be stuck up. We could have some fun."

He ran his hand down her arm and perused her body with his eyes. Tears welled in her eyes, and she turned around and darted towards the crowded room. The stranger called after her, but Jesse's feet kept carrying her forward.

Mike looked up from the bar. "Jesse, are you ok?"

Shaking her head, Jesse raced to the exit and hurried through the front doors. Paying no attention to where she was going, she bolted onto the street. Her eyes burned with tears as she stumbled into several guys heading into the club.

Jesse collided with a solid wall of muscle. "Umph."

"Shit." A deep voice muttered, grabbing hold of her body to keep her from tumbling over. Jesse flinched, jerking her body to get away. "Jess!"

Arms wrapped around her, halting her movement. "Please. Let me go." Her body shook with sobs as she tried to free myself.

"Jesse, please stop. Look at me, please, baby—it's AJ." Pressing her closer to his body, Jesse's brain caught up with the scent filling her nose and realized who it was.

"AJ? How are you here?" Jesse was sobbing uncontrollably in his arms, her tears staining his shirt with her tears.

"Hey guys, go on inside. I'll catch up with you later." Turning his head back to Jesse. "Jess, baby—take a deep breath. What happened? Did someone hurt you?"

AJ loosened his grip on her and was scanning the sidewalk. "Where's Carmen and Allie?"

Sniffing, she squeaked out, "Inside—no one hurt me. This man wouldn't leave me alone... I just freaked out. This was too soon. I shouldn't be here."

The effects of her drinking suddenly hit her hard, and she swayed on her feet. "Damn, Jess—you're drunk. You don't look so good."

"I just want to go home..." She looked like a mess standing on the sidewalk crying.

AJ scooped her into his arms. "AJ, what are you doing? Put me down!" She screamed at him, wriggling in his arms.

"Jess, you are in no condition to walk. I'm taking you home." Holding her against him, he managed to fish his ringing phone out of his pocket.

"Hey. Yep... No, don't worry, I got her. I was coming in with some guys from the base when she ran into me... literally. No —I'm taking her home; she's drunk. Ok. I'll tell her. Y'all have fun." AJ ended his call and slipped the phone back into his pocket.

"Who was that?"

"Allie, she was freaking out because Mike told her you ran out. She has your purse. You left it on the bar."

The dizziness was horrible. Jesse closed her eyes and rested her head against AJ's shoulder as he walked them to his car. Jesse sensed him opening the door and setting her in the passenger seat of what she assumed was his jeep.

Cracking her eyes open as he leaned across and buckled her in, Jesse couldn't help but inhale his scent. He smelled so good, and her body was reacting to his closeness. Being drunk was messing with her brain—Jesse knew she shouldn't be feeling any attraction to her dead husband's brother... best friend or not—but she was. Forcing her eyes closed, she pretended to be asleep so he would miss her staring.

She must have dozed off during the ride because his voice startled her. "Jess, we're home. Wake up, sleepyhead." The hour-long drive helped some of the tequila burn out of her system, but she still felt muddled.

Stretching, she sat up and felt AJ staring. "AJ, thank you for bringing me home. I... I just wasn't ready for that. It was too much. I don't want men hitting on me. It makes me feel like I'm betraying Alex somehow."

She looked away, embarrassed by her admission.

"Jess, look at me, please."

Turning, she looked into his eyes. It was the first time Jesse saw how much he cared. They sat staring at each other, not saying a word.

He finally broke the silence. "Jesse, I love you. I always have. And I can't sit here and watch you drink yourself into oblivion. I know your heart is broken. You loved him—hell, I loved him. But enough is enough. It's killing me to see you like this."

His words hit her, making her turn her head away. Pushing open the door, she stumbled from the jeep and hurried towards the front door. As she started up the steps, a wave of dizziness caused her to lose her balance. Just as she tumbled back, strong arms were there to catch her.

"Damn, Jess. I got you... hang on."

Scooping her up, AJ carried her through the front door. He kicked the door closed and navigated the steps with her in his arms. He carried her straight into her room and set her on the bed. The room was still dark as he laid Jesse down.

"Here you go." Stroking the loose hair from her face, "God, Jess. Even drunk, you're beautiful."

"Don't... I'm such a mess. AJ, you don't deserve this. You should be out dating—finding love. Not taking care of a broken-hearted widow."

Cupping her face with his hands, "Jess. I am right where I want to be. And I have love... I don't need to date. What I want is right here."

They stared at each other, never breaking eye contact. Overcome with emotion, Jesse leaned into him and pressed her lips to his. AJ's body stiffened, but soon, his lips began to move against hers. His hand tangled into her hair as he deepened the kiss. Coming to his senses, AJ broke the kiss.

"Wait... Jess, stop. You're drunk—you don't want this. You're confused right now."

Running his hands through his hair, he squatted on his heels at the side of the bed.

"AJ—I'm sorry. I...." Tears spilled from her eyes as she buried her face into her pillow to hide her embarrassment.

AJ reached out and brushed his palm down her arm. "Look, I love you. More than I think you're ready for, Jess. But when you are ready... I'll be here waiting. And when you finally decide you want more with me—it won't be after you've drunk your sorrows away. It'll be because your heart is ready. Ok?" He pulled the pillow away from her face. "Look at me.

Do you understand what I'm saying? The hardest thing I will ever do is walk out of this room tonight."

Nodding her head, "I understand. Thank you, AJ... for everything. I don't deserve you."

Standing, he leaned down and placed a kiss on her head. "You don't deserve to be a widow. You don't deserve to be sad. But Jesse, you *do* deserve to love again—when you're ready and your time. Get some rest. We'll eat breakfast together in the morning."

AJ pulled the covers over her before leaving the room. Walking out, he paused at the door. "Jesse, I've loved you since our sophomore year of high school. My brother stealing your heart didn't change that—I'd wait an eternity for you to love me like you did."

Chapter Seven

THE SUN PEEKED through the blinds, waking Jesse from her restless slumber. Dreams of tangled memories filled her night, leaving her confused and feeling guilty. Glancing at the clock, she noticed it was a little after nine in the morning. Rolling over, she placed her feet on the floor and stood. The remnants of the tequila made its presence known in them as her head throbbed from the splitting headache left over from her night out.

Moving slowly, she made her way to the bathroom. The reflection in the mirror staring back was no less than gruesome. Jesse's make-up was smeared across her skin like a two-dollar hooker that had been caught in the rain. And her hair resembled something an animal might nest inside.

Attempting to run a brush through her hair, Jesse gave up and settled on a ponytail. She quickly washed her face—scrubbing away the remnants of her failed attempt out. After brushing her teeth, Jesse returned to her bedroom and found a pair of shorts and a tank top to change into.

Glancing at the flag sitting carefully on her nightstand, thoughts of Alex washed over her. It was a constant reminder of what she'd lost. Thinking of Alex, Jesse couldn't help conjuring AJ in her mind. Instinctively, she brushed her fingers over her lips. She could still feel his lips, and her mind wandered back over what he said.

AJ loved her... he'd made that clear last night when he said he never stopped loving her and that he'd wait an eternity for me to love him back like she used to. But thinking over his admission, Jesse knew she'd never stopped loving him. She'd simply fallen in love with his brother more. Walking to the nightstand, Jesse picked up the flag and pressed it to her chest. She inhaled the musty odor, confirming a long time had passed since she was handed the only remaining tie to Alex. Reaching for the dog tags that hung over the material, she fingered the engraving. This was all she had left of him, along with memories. It was past the time to move on with life. Alex would've wanted her to, but it still felt like a betrayal. Sliding them off the nightstand, Jesse moved them to the dresser. She wasn't ready to let him go completely, but she needed to start the process of healing. Having the visual reminder of Alex by the bed made trying to move on painful.

As she started out her door, she sent a silent prayer for him to give her a sign it was ok to take a chance. As she made her way down the stairs, she could hear AJ in the kitchen. Taking a breath, Jesse worried that AJ would act weird after she'd kissed him drunk. While the liquor had driven her to act so recklessly, deep down, Jesse knew she'd wanted to feel again, and kissing him seemed so natural.

Jesse entered the kitchen, happy to find AJ at the counter. He must've heard her because he turned, shooting her the biggest smile. "Morning. How's that head of yours?"

"Ugh... I'm paying for all I drank last night. No more tequila for me!"

"You hungry? I made pancakes."

Moving to sit at the table, Jesse smiled. "Sure thing, Chef AJ. Thanks."

He carried over a plate of hot pancakes and sat down across from her. Dishing out several on Jesse's plate, AJ passed the syrup and watched as she drenched the hot stacks in sweetness. Shoving a forkful into her mouth, Jesse couldn't help but moan from the explosion of tastiness hitting her tongue. "Oh my god, AJ, these are delicious."

"Damn, if I knew making pancakes would get you to moan like that... I would have made them weeks ago."

Inhaling in shock at his response, Jesse started choking on my food. "AJ."

"Sorry. Didn't mean to make you choke. What do you have planned for the day?"

It was weird that he seemed to be avoiding any mention of the kiss they'd shared, and Jesse wasn't sure if she should bring it up. "Nah, I'm good. You just caught me off guard. I gotta grade papers, do some laundry... yep, a real exciting Saturday."

Standing, Jesse carried her plate to the sink, but out of the corner of her eye, she saw AJ stand. He made his way over and stood behind her. Jesse could feel his body heat as he leaned in close, pressing his firm chest into her backside. The heat of his breath tickled her skin as he lowered his mouth to her ear.

"I told you I'd wait until you were ready. But if you keep dressing like this," he trailed his finger down her exposed skin., "I'm going to have a real hard time restraining myself."

He made no effort to hide the arousal pressing into her back-side. Jesse closed her eyes and took a formidable breath as she dropped her dish and spun to face him. "What do you mean, dressed like this?"

Caging her against the counter, AJ ran his hand up Jesse's arm and slid his finger under the strap of her tiny tank top. "In this little tank top showing off your perfect figure, my restraint is on thin ice. My body responds to the mere sight of you. Jesse and I want to rip those teensy shorts down and bury myself inside you."

Jesse inhaled sharply as she bit her lip. Digging deep inside herself, she pushed aside her fear and pressed into him. "I guess I could take it off?"

She was scared she was making the wrong decision to cross the invisible boundary between them. Still, she needed to see how far she could take it without freaking out—and seeing the fire in his eyes, Jesse couldn't deny she loved the attention, despite flirting with danger.

"Jess... unless you're ready, you should refrain from saying something like. It will lead to things ending in you out of clothes." He stepped back to put space between them.

Jesse didn't want that, so instead, she grabbed the front of his shirt and pulled him towards her. Catching him off guard, she pressed her lips to his, making him stiffen. What started as a soft kiss soon turned into a wildfire blaze with no hope of putting out. AJ's tongue parted her lips, diving into her mouth like a man starved. Jesse wove her fingers through his hair, holding him firmly in place. They were so lost in one another that they didn't hear the front door open.

"Hey Jess, you home?" John had let himself inside once again.

Jesse spun out of AJ's hold, turning towards the sink just as John walked into the kitchen. AJ leaned around her and dumped his dish in the sink. She hated how she reacted, but she wasn't ready to face her brother yet. She appreciated AJ trying to make it look like nothing was going on.

"Um, am I interrupting something?" John's expression was one of scrutiny as he eyed the two of them.

"Nope, just finishing up breakfast. Jess... I'll catch you later. I need to shower and head to the base. I'm giving some recruits a ninjitsu lesson today." He turned, shaking John's hand as he walked by him. "I'll be back around five. See ya around, John."

John stood, staring at Jesse with his hands in his pockets. "So, Jess... what the hell is going on?"

She leaned onto the counter and shrugged. "What? We were eating breakfast."

"It didn't look that way to me when I walked in. Jess, I don't want you to get hurt or do something you will regret."

Snorting, Jesse pushed off the counter and started toward him. "Regret? What's that mean?"

"Damn it, Jess... Can you seriously stand there looking at me and tell me nothing is going on between you two?"

She stood unmoving, staring at her brother as she searched for the words. He was right—she couldn't lie to him, but she didn't know how to answer him without sounding like a nut job. "Alex has been dead for over a year—or have you forgotten that? I feel so dead inside, and AJ... well, I am feeling less dead with him. I loved him first, and I don't think that part of me ever stopped. I just fell in love with his brother more."

John walked towards her and pulled her into a hug. "I didn't mean to upset you, baby sis. I am just worried about you. I don't want AJ taking advantage of you—we all know he loves you. Hell, he always has. I only want it to be your choice and not one that comes from grief or loneliness." John leaned back and looked at her with sincerity in his gaze. Placing a kiss on her head, he released Jesse from his embrace. "Alex would want you to be happy."

"It is my choice. AJ didn't force anything on me. I kissed him last night—Somewhat alcohol induced. And you know what? He was the perfect gentleman. He told me he wouldn't push a relationship with me—that it was my decision, and I controlled what happened between us."

"Well, that makes me feel better. But do you want a relationship with him? Jess, it's Alex's brother." He raised an eyebrow, concern marring his expression.

Jesse looked down at her feet, confusion swirling inside her chest. He was right—AJ was Alex's brother... but he was also just a man—a man I loved. Not to mention, I'd known him even longer than Alex. When she thought hard about it, Jesse knew that AJ had always been in her heart. When she lifted her eyes, John was still watching me.

"Yeah, maybe it is a bit weird that it's Alex's brother. But I love him. Maybe not always in the same way as Alex—but now... I think I'm falling in love with him. He takes care of me even knowing that I am mourning his brother. Does that make it wrong? I don't know, but I know I'm lonely. And maybe it's selfish to say that having AJ here makes the pain less. John, I'll always miss Alex. But I can't help that I love AJ. And letting myself love him doesn't mean I'll stop loving Alex."

"It sounds like you've thought about things. And I know you'll always love Alex. I support you in whatever you decide. Besides, AJ has always pined for you—it makes sense that he would love you and want to take care of you. But if he hurts you. Well... I can't say I won't kick his ass."

"Yeah, fine—you can go all big brother on him. But this is AJ you're talking about—he won't hurt me. Besides... I could hurt him."

Jesse followed him as he walked towards the front door. "Come for dinner tonight. Bring AJ with you—I'm grilling steaks. Allie's still sleeping off her hangover, but she'll want to see you. She was worried after you left."

"I thought she was the designated driver... How'd she make it home?"

"She took an Uber—and by Uber, I mean me. Carmen went home with someone she met at the bar."

"Wow... alright then. I'll be there later. Maybe I'll bring some beer with me—I hear it's the best cure for a hangover."

Giggling as she stood in the open door, "And John... Thanks for being the best big brother a girl could ask for."

"Anytime, Jess! See you later." He strode across the lawn, making his way into his house. Closing the door, Jesse made her way up the stairs, stopping when she noticed AJ's door cracked.

She couldn't help but peer into the room. Her breath hitched when she found him facing the window, wrapped in only a towel. The lines of the muscles on his back looked as though Michelangelo himself had chiseled them. His legs peeked out from the white material—and man, what a nice pair of legs.

They were thick and sturdy... the kind of legs strong enough to hold someone up as he plowed into them against a wall. The towel hung low on his hips, giving Jesse a peek at the top of his perfectly tight ass. God, he was beautiful. Just the sight of him had her clenching her legs together. He turned, his gaze landing on mine. She was frozen to the spot for a moment, but when his expression morphed into a smirk, she jumped.

"Shit." She stumbled back and bolted to her room. Jesse was mortified that he'd caught her staring at him practically naked. Hurrying into the bathroom, she slammed the door shut and locked herself inside.

"Jess, you ok in there?" His voice filtered through the door. "You didn't have to run, Jesse. I would've been happy to give you my towel for your shower." His laughter resonated through the bathroom door.

"No—Oh my god. Just go away... I am embarrassed enough; don't make it worse," She groaned, pressing her head against the door.

"Well, if you want me to give you a real peep show, let me know."

"Yeah, yeah..." She shook the mental image of him naked. The last thing she wanted was to think about him in his birthday suit. "Hey, John invited us for dinner tonight. Will you be back by six?" She changed the subject, praying her mental image of his body would go away.

"I'll be back by five. I'd love to go. Oh, and Jess?" He called out to her.

"Yeah?"

"Make sure you get all clean—that way, there won't be any confusion when you get *dirty* tonight."

She heard the door close, leaving her completely lost for words.

Fuck.

She was in trouble.

Chapter Eight

AFTER SHOWERING, Jesse gathered all her laundry and headed towards the garage. The washer and dryer were outside, making laundry fun in the winter. Fortunately, it was late fall, so the temperature wasn't too bad. She started a load and found herself sitting on the couch grading papers. It wasn't uncommon for her to sit in front of the TV and do work. Most of Jesse's students were at a higher level of expertise in writing, so grading their work was easy.

Setting aside the stack of finished papers, she stretched out on the couch. She still had a couple of hours before dinner with her brother, so she opted for a quick nap to refresh herself. Laying on the couch, her mind drifted back to high school memories. She and AJ were always together in school. He'd been there for her through her dad's death and then again for her mom's. When she finally met Alex, their friendship remained intact. However, there was a time she worried AJ couldn't handle her being with his brother. She always wondered why AJ never settled down, but now, selfishly, she was thankful he hadn't. Otherwise, Jesse would be alone, dealing with the loss of Alex.

Waking to the sun setting, Jesse glanced at the clock, realizing it was five-thirty. "AJ, you home?"

The house remained silent. Standing and stretching from her spot on the couch, Jesse walked to the door—noting that AJ's car wasn't in the driveway. Odd, since he had mentioned he would be home at five. Grabbing her phone from the counter, Jesse dialed his number. His voicemail picked up after the second ring, so she left a voicemail.

"AJ, it's Jess. You said you'd be home at five. Call me back."

Ending the call, Jesse went upstairs and changed clothes for dinner at her brothers. She pulled on a sundress and slipped on some flip-flops. She was pulling her hair into a ponytail when she heard her name being called from downstairs.

"Jess? Where are you?" It was John.

"Damn, I said I'd be there at six..." She came down the stairs to see him standing by the door. His expression was frantic as he looked at her. "John, what the hell? Are you ok?"

"Jess—I need you to come with me."

"You're scaring me. What is it? Is it Allie?"

"No... fuck... Jess. Just get in the car." He reached out and grabbed her arm.

"Damn it, John." She jerked free. "What's wrong? Why do I need to get in the car? Where the fuck is Allie?"

"Jess—it's AJ. He's been in a wreck, and we need to go."

Jesse's entire world stopped, and she wavered on her feet—dizziness consuming her as the blood rushed through her ears.

It was like a jet engine was blasting through her head, deafening her to the sounds around her. She saw that John's lips were moving, but nothing was coming out.

"Jess—please snap out of it. We need to go to the hospital, ok?"

John grabbed her arms, shaking her out of the trance she was trapped in. Allie had entered the door behind him and wrapped her arm around Jesse. "Come on, Jess—let's get in the car. I'll help you."

The words came out like a whisper. "What happened?" Jesse asked as Allie eased her into the back seat.

"I don't have all the details yet. A drunk driver t-boned AJ. His passenger side took the brunt of the impact, but the jeep rolled over a few times." Driving as he spoke, "I don't know much more other than he was life-flighted from the scene. Jess, they do that on roll-overs as a precaution so that it could mean nothing, ok?"

Jesse stared out the window, tears silently rolling down her cheeks. Squeezing her eyes shut, Jesse's mind immediately flashed back to Alex's funeral. Her breath caught as she thought of losing AJ—she couldn't bury someone else she loved. Letting out a sob, she cried harder.

"I can't go through this again. I can't lose him."

Allie turned to face her from the front and grabbed her hand. "Jess, he will be fine. AJ is strong."

Nodding her head, Jesse prayed she was right—her heart was a glass shell, and losing AJ would shatter it completely.

Leaving nothing but shards of broken dreams in its wake.

The drive to the hospital felt like it took an eternity. As they pulled into the emergency room parking lot, Jesse opened my door before he stopped the car.

"Fuck—Jesse, wait!"

John shouted her name as she ran towards the entrance. She needed to get to AJ and see for herself that he was alive. The nurse at the counter saw Jesse as she ran through the doors. The nurse greeted her just as she made it to the counter.

"Hello. Can I help you? Do you need a doctor?"

"No—um, they brought my friend in by life flight. AJ Holt. I *need* to see him."

The words came out in frantic tones. Her breathing made it appear she was near a full-blown panic attack, making the nurse quirk a brow. "OK—take a deep breath. Let me see where he is. Do you want to sit over there and wait while I check?"

"No, I don't want to fucking sit! I want you to take me to him right *now.*"

"Jess, calm down. Let her do her job." John walked up behind her and wrapped his arms around Jesse.

"Damn it. Let me go. I need to see AJ." Jerking from his grasp, Jesse leaned over the nurse's station. "Go. Find. Him. Now."

"Shhhhh, Jess, please, honey—calm down." Allie was by her side, pulling her from John's hold and pressing her into her chest. "She's going to help us. Stop yelling."

"Allie, I can't lose another person. I won't survive. ... oh god, he doesn't know how I feel about him." Burying her face into Allie's shoulder, Jesse let the tears out.

Allie pulled away and wiped the loose strands of hair from Jesse's tear-stained face. "Oh—Jesse... do you love AJ?"

Nodding, Jesse looked at her feet in embarrassment. "Yes—I... I've fallen in love with him and been too afraid to admit it to him... or myself. I was embarrassed because Alex had only been dead for a year. I feel so guilty—but now... oh god, Allie, what if he is hurt badly?"

"Don't talk like that. Let's wait until the nurse goes back and finds out. Then we'll know what's going on. Ok?"

Allie guided her to the waiting room. Just as they sat down, the nurse appeared. "Mrs. Holt? Follow me, please," she waved Jesse towards her, "The doctor will talk with you back here."

"The doctor? Please tell me... is he ok, or is he dead?"

The nurse looked at her with a sympathetic gaze. "He's not dead—but he's hurt. The doctor can explain more to you. I can only take one of you back now, but the rest can come back as soon as we move him to a room."

"Go, Jesse, he'll want to see you first. Get us when he's in a room. We'll be here waiting for his parents to arrive, ok?"

"Ok."

She hugged John and turned to follow the nurse through the double doors. She led me down a corridor through the back. As they stepped to the closed curtain, she turned to Jesse and spoke. "Look, he suffered some pretty nasty injuries, so we have him heavily sedated, and he looks worse than it is. He's lucky to be alive. So, don't freak out when you see him... he'll heal."

She dragged the small room's curtain back, and Jesse couldn't stifle her shocked gasp. AJ was lying on the bed, still bloody and *very* bruised. He had several IVs and machines attached to him, monitoring his vitals. His arm was in a splint, and one of his legs was in a cast that ran from his foot to his thigh. His eyes were blackened and slightly swollen, along with tiny cuts that adorned his face.

"Oh, AJ."

Jesse ran to his side, taking his free hand in hers. "I'm here, baby—please wake up." Pressing her lips to his knuckles, she glanced over at the nurse. "When will he wake up? Can he even hear me?"

"Yeah, he can hear you, but he is heavily sedated, so it could be hours before he regains consciousness. The doctor will be here in a few moments to discuss his injuries and such. Here," she slid a chair next to the bed and motioned for Jesse to sit, "Hold his hand and talk to him while you wait. If you need anything, press the call button."

"Thank you. I'm sorry I was so rude."

"Don't sweat it. I'd be freaked out too if someone I loved was hurt and in the hospital."

Nodding, she watched as the nurse pulled the curtain closed. Taking a deep breath, Jesse turned back towards AJ and fought back her tears. He looked terrible, but he was alive—and that's all that mattered. Holding his hand, Jesse closed her eyes and prayed. His body was battered and broken, but deep down, she knew he'd pull through—he had to. The doctor sedated him to help him recover—the wires and IVs made him look so much worse than it was... at least, that's what she told herself to keep from completely losing it.

"Ms. Holt?" a deep voice startled her from her thoughts. As she turned, she noticed an older man wearing scrubs standing behind me.

"That's me, but please, call me Jesse."

"I'm Dr. Branson, the doctor assigned to Mr. Holt's case. I want to discuss his injuries and what to expect. Are you ok... to listen—or would you like someone else in here when we talk?"

"I'm ok, but can you see if his parents are here?" as she spoke, a nurse led in his dad.

"Oh my God, AJ." His dad rushed past the doctor, standing beside Jesse and AJ's bed. "What happened exactly?"

Placing her hand on his arm, "Dad, this is Dr. Branson. He was just about to tell me about AJ's injuries and prognosis."

His dad's expression broke her heart—she could see the worry of losing another son weighed heavy on his mind. Pulling him into an embrace, Jesse held on as they turned to face the doctor.

Chapter Nine

"OK. TELL US, please. What's his prognosis?" his father's voice cracked as he asked for some explanation.

"Please, sit." He motioned them to the chairs at the edge of the bed. "First, what I can tell you is that a drunk driver hit AJ. His jeep took the impact on the passenger side, forcing it to roll multiple times. Fortunately, AJ wore his seat belt, but the force crushed the side inward. While the roll bars protected AJ from head injury, he sustained multiple injuries. The fire department had to cut him out when they arrived."

The doctor paused, looking between AJ's dad and Jesse, "Now for the injuries he sustained... AJ has a broken leg, twenty stitches in his left forearm, a concussion, and suffered a lacerated spleen. We repaired that in surgery right after he arrived. As I said, he is *fortunate* to be alive. He will have to stay in the hospital for a few days, but I feel he'll make a full recovery with some time."

His dad rubbed his hand down his face, exasperated by the news. "Will he be able to return to full duty in the Navy?"

"Yes, after his cast comes off, he should be back to full duty—until then, light duty. We've already communicated with his superiors. They arrived a little before you. They are outside in the waiting room if you need to talk with them."

"Dad, I'll go out and talk with them and give them the update."

Jesse touched AJ's arm, kissing his cheek before turning and walking out of the room. She stopped just outside the door, leaning against the wall, and ran her hands through her hair. AJ *was* alive. Breathing deeply, she pushed off the wall and went to the waiting room.

Jesse saw AJ's mom pacing nervously, tears staining her face. "Mom," Jesse called out, pulling her into an embrace as she stood. "He's ok, Mom. He's ok." Betty cried against Jesse's shoulder, her tears falling as they held each other and cried.

"Mom, go see him—I need to talk with his superiors and give them the update."

Kissing her head, Jesse pointed her to the door leading to the back where he was. Turning, Jesse scanned the waiting room. In the far corner, She spotted two uniformed naval officers. Making her way towards them slowly, the butterflies in her stomach began fluttering overtime. This was the first time she'd seen any of the Naval Commanders since Alex's funeral.

Taking a deep breath, she smiled and got their attention. The older of the two stood and approached, meeting her halfway. "Mrs. Holt," he extended his hand, "Lieutenant Commander Wynn."

Jesse's heart stopped, causing her to lose her balance. She was overcome with sheer emotion and stumbled into him. "Ma'am, are you alright?"

"Yes," Quickly righting herself, she shook from the shock of hearing his name. "I'm sorry—did you say Wynn?"

"Yes, have we met?"

"Well, not officially—while I'm sure you were at my husband's funeral, I recently received your letter in the mail."

"Oh, I'm sorry. I assumed when they told me Mrs. Holt was in back with AJ, I thought he'd gotten married, and I hadn't heard. I apologize for my error."

Blushing, Jesse guided him to the seats nearest and sat down. Studying his face, she could see the lines of age. He had short, cropped hair that was gray, but he was in great shape for an older man. His muscles were visible beneath his uniform. He had a very regal presence about him, and it made Jesse feel at ease.

"First, let me thank you for sending me that letter. It was a shock but very much needed. I loved Alex with all my heart, losing him..." tears welled up in her eyes, "well, it's something I struggle with daily."

"Yes—I imagine it is hard. He was a fine soldier and friend. I'm glad the letter helped you. I was worried about sending it, but I knew it belonged to you deep down. Anyway, enough of the sad stuff. How's AJ?"

"Alive. Thank god." shaking her head, Jesse wiped the tears spilling onto her cheeks. "I... I don't know what I would have done if he had died."

Jesse looked towards the doors leading to his room. Blinking away her tears, she thought about how close she'd come to losing someone else. Lt. Commander Wynn must have seen the worry on her face because he had placed a hand over mine.

"I hope this isn't too forward of me, but are you in love with AJ?"

Turning to look into his eyes, "Yes, I love AJ—a lot more than I was willing to admit. And the letter you sent me was necessary, in all honesty. I loved Alex and still love him. But I want to move on, and the letter just reiterated Alex's desire for me to do that if something happened to him. AJ had always been a part of my life, even before Alex."

"Mrs. Holt, you're an amazing woman. I can't imagine what you've been through. AJ talks so highly of you—it never crossed my mind he was talking about Alex's wife. I just assumed the love he showed when he spoke was about his wife. I'm sorry, I shouldn't have said that since you were Alex's wife, but that boy loves you for sure."

"Commander... don't apologize—seriously. As bizarre as it may be, I love AJ just as much as I did Alex. I've known AJ longer than Alex, and perhaps it is meant to be this way—not that I wanted my husband to die, I'd give anything to have him here. But AJ has helped me through this, and I know he *loves* me. It's not a shock to hear you say it."

"I don't find it bizarre at all. And please, call me Jack. Love happens whether we are ready for it or not. Don't let fear or guilt keep you from doing something that will be good for you. Now, tell me about AJ. How is he?"

"Well, he's pretty messed up." She couldn't help but laugh. "Sorry, it's just so surreal that this is happening. AJ will be out for a while—and I know it will eat him up inside. He lives and breathes the Navy."

"He doesn't have to worry—his position is secure with us. We just want him to get better. We want to move him to the Naval

Hospital. We can rehab him there and get him back to himself."

"They are only keeping him a few days. He was lucky. He has a broken leg, some stitches, and a mild concussion. He had to have his spleen repaired—which is why he has to stay for a few days, but other than that, he gets to come home."

"That's great news. We will need to get his rehab coordinated with the Naval Hospital. We can also get someone to come to the house to help him until he gets out of that cast. I assume he will need it."

"Not for the first couple of weeks. I plan on taking my vacation time to be there for the first couple of weeks with him. Perhaps you can have someone call me to work out the schedule? Here, let me give you my number."

They exchanged numbers and spoke a little longer. The recruits he had been teaching ninjitsu to were planning on coming by over the next few days to see him—they were worried about him and needed to see for themselves that AJ would be ok. After they finished talking, Jesse walked him towards the exit.

"Thanks for coming, Jack. It was nice to meet you in person. Please don't be a stranger now. AJ would love to see you once he's home."

"You too, Jesse. Take care of him—we need him."

"I will... I realize I need him, too."

Smiling, she turned to see his mother standing at the door leading to the back. "Jesse."

"What is it, mom? Did something happen?" She ran toward her and grabbed her hands.

"No. It's... He's awake. AJ is awake, and he's asking for you, Jess."

Rushing through the doors, Jesse practically sprinted down the hallway to his room. She stopped at the open door to find the doctor and his dad standing beside AJ, talking to him.

"AJ, as I was telling your dad, your recovery will take a few months, but it will be 100%. You should have no residual damage in your leg or arm."

His voice was so strained. "Thanks, doc. Dad, what happened? I remember driving home from the base... I think someone hit me on the side."

Still unnoticed, Jesse stood against the door, watching him and listening to AJ talk. The tears ran down her face—she was relieved to see him awake and just stood, absorbing the sound of his voice. Her heart clenched just thinking about what could have happened.

"Yeah, they said your jeep was t-boned by a drunk. You flipped several times. The fire department had to cut you out, AJ— you're damn lucky to be here. We thought we'd lost you when they called and told us."

"Nah—I'm too hard to kill. But my jeep, is it totaled?"

"Seriously, son? The jeep? You almost die, and you ask about the damn Jeep? Yes. It's totaled. AJ, do you hear me? We thought you were dead. Jess, your mom, me... we thought we'd be burying another loved one." His dad got choked up on his last words.

"Dad. I'm here. I'm going to be fine. Wait—*fuck*. Where's Jesse? Is she ok?" His eyes searched the room, looking for her.

Stepping out from the shadows, his gaze landed on her, and his expression morphed into relief. His smile melted her fears away as she stepped around the doctor and approached the bed. "Jess, oh god—are you ok?" AJ reached for her hand, lacing his fingers with hers.

"AJ, you're laying in this bed and asking about me? You are nuts. You know that?"

"Jess... I just worry about you. I don't want you sad, and I can only guess how you felt when you got this call." He motioned to himself, lying in the bed.

Jesse inhaled his scent as he pressed his hand against her face, letting her tears trickle across his fingers.

"Jess, please stop crying—I'm here. I'm not going anywhere."

He pulled Jesse towards him, causing her to fall on the bed. "Shit, AJ, I could hurt you."

"Nah. I'm made of steel, remember, plus—these drugs make me feel nothing."

Sitting on the edge of his bed, so close to his body, Jesse sighed and shook her head. "I am so glad you're awake. I thought... I thought—"

"Shhhhh, Jess, it's ok." AJ turned to his dad and the doctor. "Do you think you could give us a minute alone?"

"Yeah, son—I need to see your mom and make sure she isn't losing it in the waiting room," squeezing Jesse's shoulder, "Jess, we love you, and we need you to be happy too. AJ, take it easy."

Jesse looked up at him, shocked at his honesty. "What do you mean by that?"

"Jess, I'd be a blind fool not to see your love for AJ. It makes sense—you loved him first. And we love you both. So, whatever is happening between you two... I just wanted to say it's okay. His mother and I have seen it coming for a while now. Don't be afraid of what you're feeling. When you come this close to losing someone again, it makes you realize life is fleeting—don't hide from something that could be the best next chapter in your life. We love you both."

The doctor had already left, so when his dad walked out, it left Jesse and AJ alone in the small room. She stared at the door he exited through, lost in thought about his words.

"Jess, say something. Are you ok?"

Turning, her eyes locked onto AJ's. "I'm fine. Just shocked... and confused about everything."

"Well, he's right. Life's too short to waste any time. Come here and get closer." AJ tugged Jesse until she was lying beside him on the tiny bed.

"AJ, there's no room for me. I shouldn't be lying here like this. What if I hurt you?"

"The only thing that could hurt me is never having the chance to see or feel you again. Jess, I'm sorry that I put you through this."

Propping herself to look into his eyes, she said, "Don't you dare blame yourself. This was not your fault, AJ. I'm glad you're alive—and I plan to take care of you until you are 100%. This made me realize everyone was right—even Alex knew what was best. He knew I needed to move on and live again. And I plan to do just that. I'm ready."

AJ sat stunned in silence, just staring at Jesse. He reached up, fingering a loose strand of hair against her face. "What are you saying, Jess?"

She didn't respond—Instead, she leaned forward and pressed her lips to his. AJ's fingers moved through her hair, pulling her flush against him. Careful not to hurt him, Jesse stopped resisting and leaned into his body.

"Damn, woman. That... was amazing. I think I've died—that's what it is. This isn't real." He shook his head, trying to understand what was happening.

Leaning down again, Jesse pressed her lips to his once more. "No—this is very real, AJ. I almost lost you, and it made me realize I was hiding my feelings out of guilt, mostly. I love you and always have. But I love Alex too, and always will. I can't keep pining over him like he's going to return."

"Jess—are you sure you're ready for this? I love you. You know that. But I want this to be real... for you to love me more than a friend."

"AJ, I do love you—but I'll always love Alex. He's the past, and you're my future... if you can understand that."

He pulled her lips to his. "Yeah, I think I do. I'll never try to replace my brother in your heart, Jess. I love him too, and part of me feels guilty for loving you—but I can't help what I feel."

They kissed again, wrapped in each other's arms. They didn't hear anyone come into the room. "Um, sorry to interrupt." His mother stood in the doorway.

Burying her head into the crook of his arm, Jesse tried to hide her embarrassment. AJ spoke, "Mom, you're not interrupting anything."

"Jesse, can I talk with you outside?"

Lifting her head, she looked at AJ confusedly. "Sure."

Pushing herself up, Jesse stood and made her way around her into the hall. "AJ, your dad and I are leaving. Hurry and get yourself home. We'll help you get settled once they release you. I'll be by tomorrow to check in on you, ok? I love you, son."

"I love you too, mom."

Chapter Ten

JESSE STOOD FACING AWAY from the door as his mother came out. "Jesse." She placed her hand on Jesse's shoulder.

"Mom, I know what you're going to say. He's your son, and I've betrayed him, right?" She couldn't stop the sob that had erupted from her chest.

She spun her around, pulling her into her embrace. "Oh, Jesse." Stroking my hair, "No... sweetheart, that's the furthest thing from what I was going to say. I was going to tell you I am so relieved you have opened your heart again—and to AJ, of all people. I know this is a lot for you to adjust to, but AJ has always loved you. He couldn't even commit to other girls—part of him never stopped feeling so deeply for you. It makes sense that he would be the one to steal your heart now. Jess, we love you. Alex would want you to be happy. And I venture to say that he's looking down from heaven, happy that his brother is the one that will protect your heart. So, don't feel guilty about that. Ok?"

"I love him, but part of me worries about what everyone will say." It was stupid, but Jesse worried about how Alex's or AJ's friends would react.

"Damn all those people to hell, Jesse. AJ's a good man—he didn't plan on losing his brother. And he would've never interfered with your marriage if Alex was still alive. I think he would have never fallen in love, though—his heart was yours back in high school. But fate works in mysterious ways. Maybe God knew this would happen and left AJ's heart free for you... knowing you would need him now."

Staring at her, Jesse couldn't help but be awestruck with this woman. She'd lost her son but spoke such truth about the situation that it made Jesse's pulse race. Betty was right—no one would have expected this, but surely, they would see their love for each other.

"You're right, mom. I'm just being silly. I promise to love AJ with all that I have. But I'll never stop loving Alex. He holds a special place in my heart forever."

She pulled her tighter into the hug. "Jess, you are the closest thing to a daughter I have, and I support you. We are overjoyed that there is a chance at love for you and AJ—despite how it came about."

"Thank you. You're the only mother I have now, and your support means the world to me."

Breaking free from her embrace, Jesse kissed her cheek. As she started towards AJ's door, Betty called out, "Jesse," she looked over her shoulder at Betty, "Take care of him. You need each other now."

Nodding, Jesse pushed the door open, walked inside, and found AJ sleeping. He looked so peaceful, even with all the tubes and wires coming off him. Quietly, she walked to the bedside and pulled the chair close. Sitting beside him, Jesse pulled his hand into hers and kissed his knuckles. "I love you, AJ."

She rested her head on the edge of the bed, securely holding his hand in hers. The steady beeping of his monitor lulled me to sleep. Her dreams were filled with him and Alex. Her heart ached for the love lost with Alex, but slowly, the fragile pieces were knitting themselves back together with the love she was opening herself to with AJ.

"Jess." A hand touched her shoulder, waking her. "Hey, sorry to wake you. I just wanted to see how AJ was doing."

Blinking her eyes to clear the sleep, she saw John standing beside her. "Oh, hey. What time is it?"

"It's about ten. The nurse said you've been asleep for a while. I told them I'd wake you. They want to move him to his real room now."

"Oh, ok." Standing, Jesse stretched her arms above her head. "He's good—lucky to be alive."

"Yeah, the guy that hit him... he didn't survive the crash. He wasn't wearing his seatbelt."

"Wow, does AJ know?" She turned to look at AJ, who was sleeping soundly.

"Nah, I doubt it. I just got word from the station. His blood alcohol level was 3.2. He didn't even feel anything. How he could drive is amazing to me—he's lucky he didn't hurt anyone else."

He shook his head, disgust marring his face. Being the sheriff of their small town, John witnessed a lot of stuff similar to

AJ's accident. He, of all people, knew how lucky AJ was to come out with only minor injuries. "Well, I hate he lost his life, but I'm relieved that AJ won't have to deal with any legal aspects of the accident."

"Jess... John?" AJ's voice barely a whisper, "What are y'all talking about?"

"AJ, glad to see you awake." John pushed past her, taking AJ's hand in a firm handshake. "Thanks for coming, John... But what are you talking about?"

"The man that hit you... he died about an hour ago from his injuries."

AJ sat, staring as he took in John's words. Jesse squeezed next to John and sat on the bed next to AJ. "AJ, are you ok?"

"Yeah—sorry. I hate to hear that. Did he have a family?"

"Yeah. A wife and son. Apparently, he had a drinking problem. His death did not surprise his wife. She said she knew it would happen one day. He refused to seek help."

"Sucks, I feel sorry for the kid. Growing up without a dad will be hard—even if he was a drunk."

"I'm glad it wasn't you that died. I don't think my sister here would have survived it. Hell, I wouldn't have survived it. You are family, AJ."

He tapped AJ's leg. "I got to head home—I just wanted to stop in and check on you two. The nurse said she would move you to a room, so let me know where that is, ok?"

"Of course. Thanks for coming," Jesse stood, pulling John into a hug, "I don't know what I would do without you."

"Same for me... AJ." John glanced at him on the bed. "Take care of yourself... and my sister. I'm glad she's finally strong enough to give love a chance. And I'm glad it's you."

AJ smiled at Jesse. "Thanks. I promise to take care of her."

"I know you will, AJ. You've always loved her from a distance. She's special, so don't mess it up, okay? You only get one chance at this."

Taking Jesse's hand in his, "I know fate played a part in this, as awful as it was. I promise to love her... and honor my brother as I do."

"Alright... I'll leave you two alone. Jess, Allie will be here with some of your things in an hour. She went by your house and packed you an overnight back. We assumed you'd stay at least tonight."

Waving to him as he left the room, Jesse turned to AJ. "AJ, do you need anything?"

"Just you, Jess... Just you."

The nurse came in a few moments later and moved AJ from the temporary room. He was in a private room. The Naval commander insisted AJ have a private recovery—so he ensured he was placed in his own room. Jesse, for one, was thankful. She planned on staying as long as she could with AJ. She'd already talked with her principal and explained everything. He granted her a leave of absence for two weeks, just long enough to get AJ settled at home and care arranged for him.

"AJ, my principal granted my time off—so it looks like you're stuck with me as your nurse for two weeks."

She smiled at him as she watched him raise his bed into a sitting position. AJ still had IVs and wires attached to him, but his color had started to return, making him look better.

"I may have to rip a stitch to get you to be my nurse longer."

He smiled at Jesse, reaching his hand out and beckoning her towards him as he patted the edge of the bed. "Come sit here."

She lowered herself to sit next to him. "Are you comfortable? Do you need another pillow?"

She started pulling the covers up around his chest, her hands slowing as they brushed past his bandaged arm.

"Does it hurt?" She lightly fingered the bandage.

"A little. I'm going to look like Frankenstein. Will you still like what you see when the bandages come off?"

"Are you serious?" Jesse quirked her eyebrow at him. "Scars are sexy as hell. And it wouldn't matter anyway—I love you for what's inside here."

She traced her fingers up his arm, coming to rest on his chest above his heart. AJ grabbed her hand. "Jess, I love you."

"I know AJ... and I am so sorry it took this accident for me to realize how I felt, too. It's an emotional struggle, you understand, don't you?"

"Jess, I don't want to replace my brother. I want to be someone you love, too. He wasn't just my brother. He was my best friend. Part of me struggles with the fact that I'm here loving you—when he should be. But it doesn't change how I feel about you."

"I want this with you, AJ. Can we take it slow... one day at a time?"

"Jess—we'll go as slow or as fast as you want. You're in control here. Plus, I'm somewhat broken right now. Look... Just having you say you love me is enough right now. That, and a few kisses here and there."

Winking, he pulled her closer, and their mouths pressed together. He slipped his tongue past her lips, tangling it with hers.

"Damn, that kiss is making me hot just watching!" Allie strolled into the room, causing them to break apart.

"Allie!" Jesse jumped up and ran to hug her. "Thank you so much for bringing me stuff to wear. And for... well, the other night, too. All this has made me realize how much I needed to start living again. I was just too ashamed to admit my feelings for AJ."

Allie smiled as Jesse looked back at AJ over her shoulder. "Well, it's about time. Honestly, Jess, we all knew this would happen. AJ has loved you forever—and you him. You just needed time to mourn Alex before you let your heart feel again. I'm only glad you did. But enough of that talk. I'm sure you've heard it enough today. I talked with Mr. Bower. He told me about your leave of absence. We will ensure your sub keeps your lessons going until you return."

"Are you serious?"

Jesse was shocked. Her colleagues were the best anyone could ask for. The fact that they would make sure the students wouldn't lose pace in class spoke volumes.

"Yep. We are all happy you've finally started to heal your heart —everyone loves you. So, it's settled... you won't have to worry about work and can focus on getting him well. We will ensure your students continue as though you're in the class. Katie is going to help as well. She's bright—she'll make a fine teacher someday."

"Wow, Allie. I don't know what to say. This is too much." Jesse wiped a stray tear that had rolled down her cheek. "Thank you, and thank everyone else, too. I will owe you guys big."

"Well, I gotta go. It's almost eleven, and visiting hours are nearly over. Call me if you need anything. The nurse out front told me you'd likely go home by the end of the week, if not sooner. So, when they release you, John and I will help get you settled. Jess, if you need to go anywhere—call me. I'll come."

Jesse leaned in and kissed Allie's cheek. "Thanks, Allie. You guys are lifesavers. I'll call you tomorrow. Shit, my phone."

Allie reached into the bag she brought for Jesse. "Here ya go. I grabbed the charger, too. It's at the bottom of the bag." She handed her the phone and left the bag on the chair near the door as she walked out.

"Alright, what do you need?" Jesse turned to look at AJ. "Are you thirsty?"

"Nah—I'm kind of tired." He yawned, smiling at her as she stood watching him.

The nurse walked in and grinned. "Ma'am, here are some blankets for the pull-out recliner. And a towel. Feel free to use his shower in there if you want." Pointing to the bathroom that was attached to his private room.

"Thanks—I think I'll just go and change. AJ, will you be ok for a few minutes?"

"Yeah, can't promise I'll be awake when you come out. The medicine's making me sleepy."

Walking to the edge of the bed, Jesse kissed him. "Sleep, baby. I'll be here when you wake."

She turned and walked to the bathroom, grabbing her bag as she did. Shutting the door behind her, she leaned against the cool wood. Jesse was beyond thankful for AJ. And though she still mourned Alex, her heart finally started to beat again.

Chapter Eleven

AFTER BRUSHING HER TEETH, Jesse searched her bag for something to wear. Allie had packed a pair of athletic shorts, a tank top, and several other items she might need during her stay with AJ. Pulling her hair into a tight braid, then giving herself one more glance in the tiny mirror, Jesse took a breath and stepped out of the bathroom. Tiptoeing towards the pullout recliner, she grabbed the blankets the nurse had left.

Just as she placed her phone on the table, she heard AJ take a deep breath. Spinning towards him, Jesse found him staring at her. "What? Is something wrong?"

She stepped towards him as he patted the bed. "No—nothing's wrong. Come sit with me a minute."

"AJ, you need to sleep. I need you to get better..." grabbing her, AJ pulled her into him. "What are you doing?"

His hand grabbed her head and pulled her mouth to his. The fierceness in his kiss sent chills through her body. She couldn't fight it and gave in to his demands, allowing her body to relax into his hold. Careful not to pull out his IV or hurt his leg or arm, Jesse slid into the bed next to him. Her hand traced his chest muscles, and her fingers moved down his shoulder, stopping just above his injured arm. "AJ—we shouldn't be doing this." She leaned back to look at him. "You could hurt yourself. I could hurt you."

"Jess..." his lips found hers again as he poured his emotions into the kiss.

Jesse gasped at the feel of his erection and nearly fell off the bed, moving away from his body. "AJ!"

"Do you see what you do to me? Waking up to see you in those tight little shorts and tank top. Damn..."

"AJ, I think the drugs are messing with you. As much as I want this, you need to heal. Plus—you're lying in a hospital bed."

She got out of the bed, but he grabbed her around the waist. "You're right. I'm sorry—I'm not thinking straight. Don't go, though. Will you stay here with me for a while? I'll behave. I promise."

"OK. Just till you fall asleep, you need space to rest properly."

Jesse snuggled against AJ's good side as he wrapped his arm around her and pulled her tightly to him. "I feel like I'm dreaming. If I am, I don't want to wake up."

"AJ, this is real—I'm real. GO to sleep. I promise I'll be here when you wake up."

His breathing evened out. Soon, the only sound Jesse could hear was the steady beep of the heart monitor and his even breaths going in and out. Laying there, she closed her eyes. Jesse thought about their future. Silently thanking God for sparing his life, Jesse swore to love him as long as life would allow. In the middle of the night, she was woken by a nurse who came in to check his vitals.

"Oh—I fell asleep. Let me get out of your way."

"Don't get up on my account, honey. Stay right there. I can work around you. It does him good to have you close. Touch is said to be the best healer of the sick... so stay snuggled up right there."

"Thanks. I thought I lost him..."

The nurse patted her leg. "Looks like you'll have your chance at a long, happy life. Glad it worked out. His vitals all look good. Go back to sleep."

She nestled back into his warmth, closing her eyes as she fell asleep again. Her dreams were filled with the past and the potential future. The guilt she'd felt was slowly diminishing, and her fragile heart—one she thought was a shattered ball of glass, was starting to knit itself back together again.

AJ had brought her back to life with his unwavering love. Now, it was her turn to show him the same. He was part of her past and now her future. Together, they would keep the memory of Alex alive while loving one another along the way.

The sounds of people talking stirred Jesse from her sleep. Slowly cracking open her eyes, she was pleased to find herself still wrapped in AJ's arm.

She slept here all night. I thought I was dreaming when I woke up—or had died and gone to heaven."

"AJ. Don't say something like that. We thought we'd lost you."

"Well, mom—seeing her in my arms, I wasn't sure. I love her so much. Do you think Alex forgives me up in Heaven?"

They still hadn't noticed she'd come awake, so she laid still, listening to them talk. "Forgives you? For what, AJ? Loving Jess isn't a sin—nor would Alex be mad. He wouldn't want her pining for him. It would devastate him to know she lost herself to depression. I believe he's looking down from Heaven, smiling, knowing that you are the one guarding her heart. So, stop beating yourself up over this. Live for today and love her like there is no tomorrow."

Breaking her silence, Jesse looked up into AJ's eyes. "Don't I get a say in this, too?"

"You're awake." It was more of a statement rather than a question.

"Have been for a while. I was enjoying being in your arms... rather, arm." She couldn't stifle the giggle.

"Oh, I see—you want to make fun of the injured, do you?"

"Of course not! I'm just pointing out the obvious. You only have one good arm right now." Sliding off the bed, Jesse moved toward his mom and pulled her into a hug. "Thanks for coming by."

"Well, I had to see how he was fairing today. And see if you need anything."

The door to his room opened, and Dr. Branson walked in. "Good morning. I'm glad to see you awake, AJ. How are you feeling?" He made his way to the bed and took out his stethoscope.

"I feel sore—no, that's a lie... I feel like I got run over by a fucking truck."

"AJ!" His mother and Jesse said at the same time.

It's alright, ladies. He's allowed to say that. It probably does fucking hurt." The doctor laughed as he dropped the f-bomb. "Well, your vitals are all good. Let's look at your arm and side. I need to check the sutures." He pressed the button, laying AJ flat.

Jesse and his mother watched with wonder as the doctor pulled the sheet down and lifted his gown. He gently pulled the bandage off his side, exposing two small wounds. "Well, this looks good. You'll have minimal scarring from the spleen repair. There's minimal bruising, so that means the repair was successful. Now, let's look at that arm." He pulled AJ's gown down after changing the bandage. Walking around the bed's opposite side, Jesse stood next to AJ. Taking his hand in hers, she stared at the doctor and listened. "AJ, you are fortunate to have no nerve damage. Your arm was pinned beneath the roll bar of the jeep. It's a miracle that your arm wasn't cut off."

The doctor cut the tightly wrapped gauze. Pulling it free, Jesse sucked in a breath at the sight of the damage. A long row of staples and stitches ran the length of his arm from his elbow to his armpit. The area was black and blue, with specks of dried blood littering the skin around metal teeth.

"Twenty-two stitches and fifteen staples. That's what it took to piece you back together. And believe it or not—there is no muscle or nerve damage. I attribute that to your Ninjitsu training. The muscles were flexible, making the tear more like a busted pair of pants. You almost bled to death. When the fire department got on scene, the first person to reach you tied off your artery just above the top of the gash. She saved your life."

Jesse let out the breath she'd been holding. "God—AJ."

"Doc, how long till these things come out?"

"I'd say at least six weeks. Same for the cast on your leg. It was pinned beneath the steering wheel. It was a clean break, though. We set it in the ER and put you in a cast there. It will usually heal, and I doubt you'll need much PT after. AJ, you're a lucky son of a bitch. You had a hell of a guardian angel in that jeep last night. You're doing a lot better than I expected, so if you're still doing well tomorrow, you can go home."

"Really? You hear that, babe, we're getting outta here tomorrow!" AJ's smile melted her heart.

"AJ—I'm going to head out and let your dad know the update. Jess, let me know if you need anything." His mom leaned down and kissed AJ goodbye.

"Ok, Mom, I'll call you later." Turning to the doctor after she walked out, she said, "Thanks, Dr. Branson. I'll make sure he takes it easy at home. I'll be with him for two weeks before returning to work. What restrictions will he have?"

"Mrs. Holt, he can do anything he wants. Just no walking, driving, or martial arts. But any low-level activities are fine."

"Low-level activities?" Confused, she looked at AJ for help.

"Yes. He can resume all activities as long as he's not standing. So, anything sitting or lying down is fine." He winked at AJ as silent communication passed between them.

He was talking about sex. "Oh... no, I didn't mean." Her face reddened. "Thanks for the clarification."

"Well, I'll leave you two alone. AJ—don't push yourself. Let this beautiful woman take the lead and take care of you. OK?"

"Yes, sir! Thanks again for saving my ass."

"All in a day's work. I'll stop by tomorrow. If all goes well, I'll be discharging you."

The door closed as the doctor left, leaving them alone once more. Jesse couldn't help but smile at him. "What? Why are you smiling at me like that?"

"I can't believe the doctor thought I was asking about sex... I must look like I want to jump your bones or something?"

"Nah—I think he can tell how much you love me. It's all over your face when you look at me."

Throwing a towel at him, Jesse laughed. "You seem pretty sure of yourself."

"Jess. It's the same look I have when looking at you. Come here. You're too far away from me." He reached out, wiggling his fingers.

Sitting on the edge of the bed, Jesse rested her head on his shoulder, absentmindedly tracing the ridges of his chest muscles. "AJ?"

"Yeah?"

"Do you think Alex is ok with this—with us?"

"I have to believe he would want you happy, Jess. And I pray he knows I love you and only want you to be happy again. He knew I loved you when he was alive. Didn't he ever tell you that?"

"No—he never mentioned a thing. He knew? What did he say to you?"

"Honestly?"

"Yeah—honestly."

"Alex told me he knew I loved you—but you were his. He said he was sorry that he was the one to win your heart and hadn't meant to fall in love with you. He made me promise to look after you if anything ever happened to him. He knew I would ensure the safety of your heart. I don't think he ever thought it would happen, though."

Jesse watched as a tear fell from his eye. It rolled down his chest and dripped onto her skin. "AJ, don't cry—please."

"Sorry. I know it's not manly. But—uh." AJ sighed, "I miss him, even though it would mean I wouldn't have you like this... I wish he were here."

"I know. I do too... I love you, but I'd give anything to have him back with me... with us."

AJ pulled her closer. "I love you, Jess. We will always mourn him—together. I promise to keep his memory alive for the both of us."

Snuggling into his embrace, Jesse let herself cry. They were tears of pain and happiness. She'd lost Alex. And some tears were for him—but they were also for the love she'd found in AJ. Together, they would navigate the pain they shared for a man who was lost to them both. She lay in his arms for what felt like hours, listening to the steady beating of his heart. AJ had fallen asleep some time ago, and Jesse didn't want to move out of fear of waking him.

"Jess?" Turning her head, she found Carmen standing in the doorway.

"Carmen? What are you doing here?"

"I had to come to see if you guys were ok. Allie called me yesterday. I'm sorry I didn't come sooner."

She carefully peeled herself out of AJ's hold, slipping out of the bed, trying not to wake him. He stirred but didn't open his eyes. Carmen reached out to her, pulling her into a firm hug.

Carmen cried as she held Jesse. "God, Jess, I was so worried when I got the call. I thought you'd have to bury another person. There's no way you'd come back from that. I thought I'd lose you to grief."

"Carmen—it's ok. AJ may even go home tomorrow. We'll know when the doctor checks on him later this morning."

"Thank god! So…"

"Sooo… What?"

"Are you going to give him a chance?"

Laughing at her question, Jesse nodded at what she thought was obvious. "Well, it's more like he's giving me a chance."

"Right—whatever you must tell yourself, Jess. That boy has loved you since the tenth grade." She laughed as she wiped the tears from her face.

AJ pushed himself up on the bed. "Um, hey, Carmen."

"AJ. I'm glad to hear you're going to make a full recovery. We'd miss that ugly mug of yours around Jess's house."

"Glad I can continue to give you something to stare at," he chuckled.

"Well, now that I've seen with my own eyes, you're going to be ok; I'll get out of here. Plus, there's a sexy male nurse I need to see about."

"Carmen, glad to see you haven't changed a bit." AJ shook his head as she made her way toward the door.

"You know me, always looking for Mr. Right. Jess, call me if you need anything. Allie brought me your work from school. I'll make sure it gets put in the grade book tomorrow. Take care, you two—we'll be glad when you're back home, AJ."

"Thanks, Carmen, stay out of trouble."

Jesse turned to look at AJ. "You need anything?"

"Some water would be good—maybe some food. Think they'll let me eat something other than that shitty Jell-O?"

"Dunno. Press your call button so we can ask."

After pressing the call button, the nurse confirmed he could try some food. Jesse had the orderly bring him something from the cafeteria, which was not that great—but it was better than ice and Jell-O. After he ate, they sat talking about plans for when he left the hospital. They had decided that they would have a bed moved into the back dining room. Since AJ couldn't navigate the stairs easily with his cast, she figured it would minimize that need. Jesse called John, and he promised to get everything set up for when he was released.

As night fell, she curled up against him in the tiny hospital bed. "Are you sure you're comfortable with me like this?"

"I don't think I could sleep without you, Jess." Pulling her tightly to his body, "How about you... are you comfortable?"

"Very. There's nowhere else I'd rather be."

In the dark room, they fell asleep, cradled against each other. Jesse hoped the doctor would give him the green light to go home tomorrow—they were both relieved and nervous about that prospect. Before the accident, they lived as roommates, but now... they were taking the relationship to a new level.

It would be scary, but there was no other person Jesse could see navigating the waters of love with.

AJ had been her best friend, and now he was the man who held her heart. The future was unclear, but she knew it was less frightening with him by her side.

Chapter Twelve

TRUE TO HIS WORD, the doctor released AJ the following day. Jesse wheeled him down to the car, loaded him up, and made their way home. John had gone to the house with AJ's parents to set up. Thank God John and Don were still there when they arrived because it took both of them to get him out of the car. AJ was not light, and with the weight of the full leg cast—he weighed a ton.

"Alright. I moved the big bed from the guest room down into the dining room. There's a table and a lamp as well. You can use the downstairs bathroom. Fortunately, it has an old-fashioned clawfoot bathtub, which will be best for you. You can hang your leg off the side."

"Thanks, John. I couldn't have moved the bed alone." Jesse hugged him, kissing him on the cheek.

"Jess, Betty filled the fridge with meals for the first couple of days. She will bring more later but didn't want you to fuss over dinner."

"Wow... I hadn't even thought about cooking. Thank God for your mom, AJ."

"She'll come by later today to help with anything you need."

Don looked at her brother. "John, do you mind driving me home?"

"Yeah, come on, I'll take you now. I have to get to the department, anyway. Jess, call me if you need anything. Allie will be home around four, but if you need something before then... call. I'll swing by in the patrol car."

"Yeah, you can call on me too—Betty and I are just around the corner."

Walking them to the door, "Thanks. You guys were an enormous help. I'll call if I need anything—promise."

Walking back into the house, Jesse found AJ sitting on the bed in the dining room. Scooting over, he made room for her and patted the mattress, asking her to sit beside him. "Well, we're home. You want me to move a TV in here for you?" she said, looking around the room and deciding where she could put one for him.

"I don't care about television." He fingered the back of her hair, freeing the braid from the tie that held it in place. "Right now, I just want to hold you."

Wrapping his hands in my hair, he pulled her into him. Their lips met. Slowly, Jesse adjusted her position on the bed so she was straddling him, careful not to press her weight on his cast. "Jess..." just the uttering of her name filled her body with desire.

"AJ, we need to slow down." She rolled off him and stood. "I'm going to get some lunch for us." Walking from the room,

Jesse heard his sigh loud and clear. She knew he wanted more, but she wasn't ready yet. Hell, he was only just out of the hospital—she needed to be sure she wouldn't hurt him.

She made a couple of sandwiches and carried them back into the bedroom. AJ was on the bed, fully stretched out, wearing only the athletic shorts he had put on to leave the hospital. His chest was pure perfection despite being black and blue and littered with scrapes. Her mind drifted back to the day of his accident—when she'd stood outside his door watching him in only a towel. Biting her lower lip, she groaned.

"Like what you see?" AJ said, breaking her from the erotic thought she was having.

"What?"

"You're staring at me..." he laughed. "You can come closer. I'm real, you know."

"You're funny." She made her way towards him. "I was just thinking—sorry. Here." She thrust the sandwich at him. "You need to eat."

"Sit with me. Please." he patted the empty spot next to him. "It'll be a lunch date."

Reluctantly, she sat down, and they sat in silence. Jesse couldn't help but sneak glances at him. Hell, he was beautiful, even in his current state. "Jess, um... I want to take a bath." His voice snapped her back to reality.

"Ok, I'll leave you so you can have privacy."

"Um... I don't think you understand. I can't do it alone. I need your help."

"Oh…" That would mean she would see him naked. Jesse swallowed. She wasn't sure if she was ready for that. "Ok. I don't have a choice—unless you want me to call your dad."

"Jess, I'd rather not be naked in front of my dad, but if it makes you uncomfortable—call him."

Standing there, she thought about it… that would mean she'd have to call his dad over here whenever he wanted to bathe. "No, I can do it. Let's get you up and into the bathroom." She handed him his crutches and followed him into the bathroom. "What's going to be easiest? Do you want me to start the water and help you in?"

"Yeah. But my balance isn't the greatest. Can you help me get these off?" gesturing to his shorts. Jesse gulped.

"Don't worry, Jess, I'll be a gentleman this time."

She cut the water on, letting it heat, and moved to stand before him. Jesse took a deep breath and muttered, slipping her fingers beneath the elastic waistband. "It's fine. I'm fine."

Slowly pushing his shorts down, Jesse squatted in front of him. His tight boxers and massive bulge staring her in the face left little to the imagination. Aside from feeling him in the hospital, Jesse didn't know what to expect. Glancing up at him, she saw him staring at me. "Jess, I can't get in with my boxers."

Swallowing, she shook her head no. Gripping the smooth microfiber, she slowly dragged them down. She could tell it was taking everything out of him to restrain himself. His leg muscles and butt were tense as she brushed her hand over the globes of his ass and eased the material over his cast. Trying to avoid looking, she gave in and came face to face with his very erect member.

"Sorry—I tried to think of something else, Jess. I didn't want to make this awkward for you. But damn. Having you down on your knees makes it real hard... literally."

She couldn't take her eyes off him—it was like she was a sixteen-year-old girl coming face-to-face with a penis for the first time. Blinking, Jesse slowly stood. "It's fine, AJ. I know this is awkward for you, too."

He let out a grunt. "Awkward? No, Jess, this is freaking brutal. My dick is as hard as nails in front of the woman I love—and there isn't a damn thing I can do about it. Awkward doesn't come close to describing what I feel."

"Look, this is hard for me, too." She couldn't stifle the giggle bubbling up from her gut. "Sorry, AJ. No pun intended."

Her laughter became intense, and she snorted. Tears spilled from her eyes as she giggled uncontrollably. When she finally gained composure, she looked at AJ. He was propped on his crutches, with his hands covering his dick.

"Great, you laugh the first time you see me naked. You're doing wonders for my self-esteem, Jess."

"Oh, God—AJ! I'm sorry... it's not that. I'm not laughing at your—" waving her hands at his now-covered parts. "Manhood. I'm laughing at the sheer awkwardness of this situation. Do you know how badly I want you right now? Not to mention... Damn, you're perfect. I want the first time we are together to be about us and not about me having to undress you because you can't do it yourself."

Jesse stepped close to him. "I want you to be in complete control of your entire body when we finally go there." Pressing her lips to his, "Now, do I need to help you in the tub, or can you manage?"

"I can manage—I've already given up enough of my dignity."

Smiling, Jesse turned to leave. "I will be back in a little while. I'm going to go take a shower myself."

"You could just get in with me." AJ waggled his eyebrows at her as she pulled the door closed. "You know you want to!" He hollered through the closed door as Jesse hurried towards the stairs.

Walking out of the bathroom was damn hard. Being close to him while he stood there naked reminded her just how badly she wanted him. But Jesse wanted to take their time and have him healthy when they took it to the next level.

$$Chapter\ Thirteen$$

SIX WEEKS LATER....

"AJ! Come on, we're going to be late!"

AJ was finally getting his cast off and his staples removed, and the last six weeks had been exhausting for both of them. Jesse had taken the first two weeks off to help him, and a male nurse with home healthcare had helped the last four. AJ had become good on his crutches, so showering had become much easier for him—and Jesse didn't have to strip him down... even though she enjoyed taking his clothes off.

"I'm coming already! Geez..." AJ hobbled down the hallway towards the door, "Well... are *you* ready?"

"Har-har, AJ. I've been ready. We can start to have normalcy once that thing," pointing towards his cast, "comes off."

Pressing himself against her body, "Normalcy, huh?"

Pushing him back slightly, "Whoa, big boy... take it slow, will you? Let's get in the car, ok?"

Smiling, he pushed past her, slowly making his way outside and down the steps. Dr. Branson's office was only fifteen minutes away, so the drive took no time, and there was hardly any traffic. Jesse was out on Christmas break from school, so they were both excited about having time to spend together without having to tend to him as an invalid. AJ and Jesse had taken their relationship slow. They'd exchanged a few heated kisses here and there and did some heavy petting over the last six weeks... but that was all. At Jesse's request, they were always fully dressed during any of their heavy make-out sessions. AJ wanted Jesse to be sure she was ready for that kind of relationship, and he wanted to be fully mobile—to woo her... that's what he'd said when they'd talked about the next step.

Only she didn't need to be wooed. Jesse knew she loved him. She probably always had, but Alex had stolen her heart back in school, although a small part had always belonged to AJ.

"Whatcha thinking about over there?" AJ broke the silence as they pulled into the parking lot.

"Nothing... just excited to get that stinky cast off your leg. You know you smell like a rotten hotdog, don't you?"

He laughed as she pulled the key from the ignition and got out. "Rotten hotdog? Seriously, Jess? You have my hotdog on the brain..." he winked as she shut the door. Jesse moved to his side and pulled the crutches out of the backseat. Opening his door, Jesse thrust the crutches at him.

"Bite me, AJ. Just get yourself out of the car, and let's go. Or maybe you want to stay gimpy."

They were both laughing as they entered the office. The receptionist greeted them as they walked in.

"Morning, Mr. Holt, Mrs. Holt. How are y'all doing today?"

"Aw... we're great. And I'll be even better when I get this rotten hotdog off my leg." AJ winked at Jesse as he answered the woman.

"Rotten hotdog?" She cocked her head in a questioning manner, confused as to what the joke was.

"Never mind. Let's just get this thing off!" He pointed to his now dingy cast.

"Ok—well, have a seat. Dr. Branson will be ready in a few minutes."

They made their way into the waiting room and sat down. "What if he says you're not ready to come out of that thing?"

"What's wrong, Jess? Is the cast causing *you* some problems?" His brow squished together as he cut his eyes at her.

"Umm, no... I, well... Never mind."

What was she supposed to say? *'Hey AJ, I want that cast off so we can do it?'* or better yet, *'I can't make love to you with that thing in the way.'* Jesse didn't want to come off forward or pushy, but she knew she wanted AJ.

Alex had been dead for over a year, and hell... she hadn't had sex with a man in almost two. With Alex being deployed, that part of the relationship was put on hold until he returned. And since he didn't, well... she'd been celibate.

"What? You can tell me, Jess."

"AJ, I'm just ready to move on with my life. Do you understand?"

"Oh... you're tired of having to take care of me." He sounded dejected when he answered.

"You're stupid. I love taking care of you... but—I'd rather TAKE CARE of you." Jesse emphasized it as she bobbed her head, hoping he would read between the lines.

"OH..." He was about to say something, but the nurse called his name.

"Mr. Holt, Dr. Branson is ready for you."

"Come, my lady—let's get this damn thing taken off... so we can get home, and you can *take* care of me." He smiled as they stood and followed the nurse into the back.

They were greeted by the doctor when they got back to the room. "Morning AJ, Mrs. Holt. How's all the injuries holding up?"

"They're great. Let's get this cast off so Jess will stop telling me it smells like a rotten hotdog." AJ laughed as he spoke to the doctor.

"I'm not even going to ask." Dr. Branson shook his head. "First, let's get an x-ray to be sure it's fully healed. If you would go with Tracy here, she'll get your films."

AJ hobbled out of the room with the nurse, leaving Jesse and Dr. Branson alone. "Mrs. Holt, how have you been?"

"I've been great. That nurse that you recommended for home help was fantastic! He truly helped AJ get to where he is now."

"Good, glad to hear everything worked out for the best."

AJ hobbled back a few minutes later with the Nurse in tow. "His films are in the system, Doctor."

Tracy smiled as Dr. Branson keyed something into the computer mounted on the wall. Several X-rays appeared, and he smiled. "Well, everything looks great, AJ. I'll remove the cast and remove the remaining staples in your arm. You'll be good as new."

AJ was visibly excited. "Does this mean I can start training Ninjitsu again? My recruits are eager for my return."

"I don't see why not; your leg has healed nicely. You need to take it slow your first few times back. In fact, you should be able to do whatever you want. Your injuries have healed at 100%."

"Whatever I want?"

Jesse started coughing, causing Dr. Branson to look over at her. "Geez, AJ, you're about to give this young woman a heart attack."

She took a deep breath and said, "I'm fine, just swallowed wrong."

"AJ, I'd like to see you back in a week—to ensure the leg is still good, but there is no need for physical therapy. Your martial arts kept you in such good shape that your muscles atrophied very little."

AJ grinned as he shook the doctor's hand. "Thanks, Doc, that's great news."

"You hungry?" Jesse asked him as they made their way to the car.

"Yeah, I could eat—but let's get something to go." His smile sent a shiver down Jesse's spine. He had a look of unadulterated lust in his eyes.

"You don't want to sit down somewhere and enjoy a meal?" She joked, knowing he was anxious to get back home. They'd been dancing around the physical aspect of their relationship for too long, and both were ready to combust.

.

"It's not a meal I want to enjoy, Jesse," getting into the passenger seat, he turned to look at her. "But if you want a lunch date, a few more hours of waiting to be alone with you is alright."

Gulping, "To go is good."

Jesse cranked the car and backed out. Dashing through the drive-through for some fast food, neither of them spoke. Pulling into the driveway, AJ took her hand in his. "Jess, you know I want you. I've wanted you since high school. But—" he took a deep breath and paused. "If you're still not ready—I understand."

He must have sensed her apprehension, and while she was nervous, Jesse was sure about one thing. She wanted him "AJ... I don't think you're ready for me." She hopped out of the car carrying their food.

AJ jumped out, racing after her up the steps. As she unlocked the door, he scooped her up—grabbing the food from her hands, he set it down on the entry table. "AJ!"

He kicked the door shut with his foot, spinning her around and pressing her back to the door. His lips were on hers before she could protest. Wedging his knee between Jesse's legs, AJ propped her up and fisted her hair. His kisses were hungry, and she could feel his erection pressing into her belly.

"AJ, don't hurt your leg," she whispered against his lips.

He didn't speak. Instead, he lifted her, allowing her to wrap her legs around his waist. Carrying her through the living room, AJ dropped her on the bed. "I've waited a lifetime for this."

AJ slowly climbed onto the bed, hovering over Jesse's body. He kissed and nipped at her neck, peppering her skin with his lips. "You. Drive. Me. Crazy."

Jesse grabbed his shirt, pushed it over his head, and ran her hands down his chest. She tugged at his pants—making her intentions clear. AJ jumped off the bed. "You're still wearing too many clothes, Jess."

She sat up, stripping herself of the dress she was wearing. AJ's quick intake of breath told her he liked what he saw. "I put this on in hopes you'd see it."

AJ kicked his pants off, launching himself at her on the bed. His hands wrapped around Jess's wrists as he pinned them above her head. "Like? No, I love."

He kissed her with a ferocity that left her winded. Releasing her hands, AJ trailed his fingers down her bare shoulder, pushing her bra strap off. He tugged the black lack material down, exposing her breasts to him. Taking my nipple in his mouth, he bit and sucked, eliciting a moan from Jesse.

"AJ." She struggled to speak, the rush of his touch sending shock waves through her. Jesse's center ached and dripped with his every touch.

"I love you, Jess." AJ shimmied his way down, hooking his fingers beneath the elastic of her panties. The hungry look in his eyes sent heat straight to her core. He pulled down her panties, stripping her bare. Shoving Jesse's legs apart, AJ buried his face in the apex of her thighs and inhaled the scent of her.

Flicking out his tongue, swirling around her clit with the slightest pressure, the sensation caused her to scream out. Pushing in and out of my slit, AJ slowly slipped a finger in, hooking it to find that tender spot inside. With the combination of licking and the gentle motion of his finger, Jesse couldn't hold back the orgasm that burst from her body.

She pulled at his hair, begging for more. AJ—Please... I need to feel you."

He grabbed his discarded pants from the floor and quickly joined her on the bed. Straddling her on the bed, he tore open the foil packet, sheathing his rigid member. "Are you sure?" He searched her face for an answer.

Grinding against his cock, "Yes. Make love to me."

He pushed into her wet folds, stilling for a moment as she adjusted to his size. It felt so right having him buried deep inside her. "God, you're so tight. It feels like heaven."

Jesse pushed her body against him, urging him to move. He didn't hesitate. Instead, he pumped in and out of her hole, all the while making love to her mouth with his tongue. His body found a rhythm, sending Jesse over the edge. With his cock buried deep, her walls tightened around him, and she screamed out another orgasm.

"That's it, baby, come all over me. I want to feel your pussy *own* my dick."

AJ spoke, his dirty mouth making Jesse wild. After her body stopped shaking, she forced him to roll over, putting her on top. Slowly, she sank down and began moving. Up and down in the perfect rhythm, she milked his cock. His thumb found its way to her sensitive bud. As he flicked and pinched it, Jesse felt the shock waves of another orgasm hit.

"AJ—please... oh god, I'm coming again."

His movements got faster and harder as he drove into her. "I'm going to come—is that what you want, Jess?"

"YES!" She bounced and rode him, pushing him over the edge.

With one last flick of her hips, Jesse squeezed his shaft in a vise grip. He erupted like a dormant volcano that was finally blowing. Spent, Jesse collapsed against his chest.

Kissing her head, AJ blew out a breath. "God—I love you more than I ever thought possible. Thank you, Jess. Thank you for giving me the chance to love you for real."

Jesse closed her eyes and let the post-sex exhaustion take her. She awoke several hours later to the feel of a warm body pressed against hers. AJ was sound asleep with his arm draped over Jesse's stomach.

Her chemistry with AJ differed from what She'd had with Alex. While she loved Alex, and the sex was good—but what she'd experienced with AJ was beyond that. She didn't know if it was the love she felt pouring out of AJ's soul or if it had just been so long since She'd had intimacy with anyone. Either way, it was beautiful. Watching him breathe, Jesse smiled at her second chance at happiness. AJ was perfection in so many ways. Good looking, kind, and honest—Jesse felt safe giving him the keys to her heart.

"Hey, beautiful." AJ stirred, cracking an eye open to stare at her.

"Hey, yourself." She pressed her lips to his, shifting from under his arm to deepen the kiss.

"Damn, we must have fallen asleep... what time is it?"

Glancing at the clock. "It's almost seven. Are you hungry? We didn't eat after all…"

As if on cue, his stomach thundered, "Uh… I guess my stomach answered. Let's shower and go to dinner."

AJ kissed her head and sat up on the bed. She couldn't stop staring at him—he was beautiful.

"Stop staring at me, woman. Or we won't make it to dinner." He threw his pillow at her.

"Want some company in the shower?"

He scooped Jesse off the bed into his arms, kissing her hard as he made his way towards the shower. Pushing the door open, he set Jesse down long enough to turn on the water. Jesse stepped around him and stood under the warm water, letting it cascade over her head. AJ's hands worked the soap into a lather as he moved behind me and ran his hands down her body.

"Jess… I love you."

Turning to face him, she smiled and wrapped her arms around his neck. Pulling him to her, Jesse pressed her lips to his. AJ backed her up to the shower wall. His kisses became more urgent and needy as his tongue pushed through into her mouth. AJ's hand traced down her side and slipped between her legs. His fingers found their way into her center, already dripping wet for him. Her sensitive bud throbbed with desire as he applied the slightest presser. She was screaming his name out as her body shattered from his touch.

"AJ."

He hoisted her up, pressing her against the shower wall. Jesse wrapped her legs around him, his cock poised right at her center. She groaned as the tip of his dick pressed against her opening. Mobbing her hips, she brushed against his groin, begging him to fuck her. AJ flexed his hips and slid into her. It felt like a fairytale as the warm water cascaded over their intertwined bodies. His thrusts slapping against her bare skin echoed in the stall. It didn't take long before she was seeing stars again. He called out her name as he lost control, spilling his seed deep inside her. The trickle of cum ran down her legs as he slipped out.

As her feet touched the floor, AJ spoke, breaking the silence. "God, woman, you've captured my heart and soul. I love you."

"I love you too, AJ." Her stomach growled, making him laugh. "I'm starving now—you gave me a workout."

Smiling, she stepped from his grasp, rinsing off under the stream of the water. AJ leaned against her, kissing the tender flesh beneath her ear. "I'm starved, too. Let's go out. I want to take you out on a proper date."

He brushed his thumb down her lip and leaned in to steal another kiss before stepping out.

"An actual date? I'd like that, I think. I'll go throw on some clothes and meet you back down here. Sound good?" Jesse stepped out and wrapped a towel around herself.

She cocked her head, watching him. He was beautiful, draped in just a towel. As she let her eyes trail over his muscular frame, the definition of his muscles along his chest and stomach sent awareness through her veins. The towel hung low enough, giving her the perfect peek at the thick cock shielded beneath.

"Yep—don't take too long... I could eat a whole cow. You worked my appetite up." Winking at her, he strode away to get dressed.

Jesse followed him up the stairs, watching him disappear into his room. She couldn't believe they were finally giving in to the feelings they'd ignored for so long—more so Jesse than him. The guilt still gnawed at her from deep inside, but the warmth of his love seemed to keep it from consuming her. Once he closed his door, Jesse pushed through her door and froze.

Feelings of loss consumed her as she stared at the flag sitting on her dresser. How could she feel so loved and still feel sadness?

Brushing her hand across the dusty edge of the folded flag, her finger toyed with the dog tags still draped over the fold. A lonely tear escaped her eye as she thought of Alex. Inhaling deeply, she sat on the edge of the bed.

Jesse missed Alex. The life they were supposed to have was stolen from them both. The pain of the loss and remorse rose to the surface, threatening to destroy her happiness. Laying down on the bed, still wrapped only in a towel, Jesse gave into the tears and let them fall.

Chapter Fourteen

"JESS," AJ rushed to the side of the bed, "Baby—why are you crying?"

She couldn't stop the tears from falling. Instead, she buried her head into AJ's chest. He pulled her closer, brushing his hand through her still-wet hair. "Jess, baby. Please tell me what's wrong. Did I do something? Did something happen? Jess... you're scaring me."

Shaking her head against his clean shirt, Jesse leaned back to look at him. Sucking in a ragged breath between sobs, "Alex... I —I miss him. The flag reminded me he's gone and not coming back."

"Oh, Jess..." Alex pulled Jesse against him tighter. "I miss him too. Maybe this—us... is too soon for you. I shouldn't have rushed you."

"NO—AJ... you didn't rush me." She sat up, wiping the remnants of her snot and tears away with the edge of her towel. "God, I'm a mess." AJ looked away from her, loosening his hold on her. "AJ. Look at me." She grabbed his face, forcing him to look at her. "This is not about you and me. I just had a moment—I miss him. I'll always miss him, but that doesn't mean I don't love you. I wanted you... I want us, AJ. I won't ever stop loving Alex. He'll always have a part of my heart. But YOU have my heart now—I meant what I said; I love you, AJ. I'm sorry I'm such a mess."

He sat staring at her. "I love you too, Jess. I don't expect you to forget him or stop loving him. I just want you to have enough room in your heart for me, too."

"AJ, you're the reason I haven't completely shattered. I've always loved you—and now I'm *in* love with you. All these feelings just overwhelmed me. We are good. Last night, this morning... was more than I could have asked for. It was perfect." Pressing a kiss to his lips, he said, "Let me get dressed so we can grab some food. I'm starved."

Shimming out of his lap, Jesse stood and went to her closet. Pulling on a pair of jeans and a sweatshirt, she grabbed her running shoes and stepped out to find AJ standing at the dresser. He was fingering the worn flag with tears in his eyes.

"AJ." walking up behind him, Jesse wrapped her arms around his waist. "We'll get through this together. Alex would want us to move on."

Turning towards Jesse, AJ kissed her head as he mumbled, "Do you think he forgives me?"

"Forgives you for what?"

"For loving you... and you loving me back instead of him?"

"There's nothing to forgive. I don't love you instead of him—I love you in addition to him. My heart has space for both of you. You're my present. He's my past. We don't forget the past, AJ. We move on and live in the present. Now... I'm starved! Where are you taking me on my date?"

Smiling, she grabbed his hand and pulled him from the bedroom. They walked down the steps, holding hands without speaking. There were no words needed. They were both mourning Alex but moving on despite the pain of the loss he had left behind. The weather was cool when they made it to the car. Looking towards her brother's house, Jesse saw Allie walking towards her car.

"Hey, Allie!" she said, throwing her hand up in a wave as Jesse rounded the car to the passenger side.

Allie tossed her hand up in a half wave and started towards us. "Jess, I wanted to ask if you were coming to the house for Christmas Eve dinner. You can invite AJ's parents."

"Oh. I almost forgot Christmas dinner was this weekend. AJ, what do you think? Will your mom and dad be ok with dinner at John and Allie's house?"

"They'll be fine with it... I'll call them from the car. Should we tell them to bring anything?"

"Nah—I'm going to cook everything," Allie smirked as she spoke. Her cooking was divine, so Jesse had no problems with letting her cook for them.

"Well, how about we bring dessert?" AJ asked as he opened his door.

"Sure, that will work. I'll let you guys get to wherever you're going. Call me later, and we will work out the times and stuff. We'll exchange gifts on Christmas Eve right after we eat. I swear he's like a giant kid at Christmas."

"I thought he was a giant kid year-round." Jesse laughed as she spoke, remembering some pranks John had pulled on friends at work.

Allie busted out laughing. "Well, you know he becomes a bigger kid at Christmas. I can't wait to see him as a dad."

The unmistakable twinkle in Allie's eyes told me she was hiding something, and it made me wonder if they had finally started talking about making a family of their own.

"Yeah, I can't wait to be an aunt... so you think you two can get to that already?"

"Well, you never know." With that, she turned and headed towards her car. "I gotta run, guys. See you later. Jess, I'll call you with details later."

"OK. Talk to you soon."

Getting into the car, Jesse turned to look at AJ. "Something's up with her. She seemed off."

"You think so? Maybe she's just excited to cook dinner for everyone."

"Perhaps... Speaking of dinner—I'm starved. Where are we going?"

"Well, do you think you can hold out a little while longer? I want to take you to a fusion restaurant in San Diego."

"Oh, that sounds perfect! Plus, it gives us time to chat."

"Chat? About what... are you having second thoughts?"

"Geez, AJ. Why do you automatically assume I've changed my mind about us? I am in this—I love you." Smiling, She took his hand in hers.

"I wanted to talk about sleeping arrangements in the house. Since you are cast-free, you don't have to sleep downstairs."

"Well... that's true. But I can move back into my room."

Jesse didn't respond to his comment. Instead, she sat silently, listening to music as they drove to dinner. AJ called his parents, inviting them to John and Allie's for dinner tomorrow night on Christmas Eve. The hour ride was peaceful, but she could tell AJ was worried about what she wanted to discuss. Jesse hoped he didn't freak out about what she wanted to ask him.

They pulled into the parking lot and parked. "Alright, you ready for some good fusion?"

"Most definitely!"

AJ took her hand in his as they walked into the tiny restaurant. The hostess seated them in the back at a table facing towards the coast. It was a breathtaking view. "Wow! This is beautiful."

"It is."

AJ's voice was low and husky. Turning, she found his eyes trained on her, not the view she'd been referring to. "Stop staring at me."

"I can't. You're too beautiful, and I am having a hard time believing you're here with me."

"AJ..." Jesse glanced down at her lap, embarrassment creeping up her neck, leaving her flushed.

"Jess. I love you—and I am just so damn lucky you've given me the chance to show you. I know what led us to this place is awful... hell, I'd live an eternity never having you love me like this if it meant my brother was here, but he's not. And I promise to love you enough for him, too."

She looked up to see his eyes brimming with tears, mirroring her tear-stained face. The love he felt for her was unmistakable—and overwhelming. "AJ... I don't know what to say. I love you. And because of you, I'm able to feel love again. I miss Alex every day—but with you, my heart can move on."

She reached across the table, slipping her hand in his. He reached across the table with his free hand and ran his thumb across a lone tear spilling down her cheek. "Don't cry. I can't bear to see you hurting anymore."

Smiling, Jesse shook her head. Just as she was going to answer him, the server appeared. "You two ready to order?"

"Um... AJ?"

"Why don't you just bring us the house sampler and a bottle of house wine?"

"Sure thing. I'll be right back with the wine."

AJ lifted her hand as the server left and pressed his lips to her knuckles. "Let's promise to live each day for each other—making sure we never go to bed angry and are always honest. Jess, I promise to protect your heart. Even the part that still holds love for my brother."

"You're too good for me, AJ. You've given me so much over the last year, and I don't know how to repay you."

"Just love me, Jess. Give me your heart... what's left to give of it? Ok?"

"Ok."

Dinner arrived, and they sat talking about their fond childhood memories. They talked about Alex and all the things they loved about him. AJ was her future—whatever that held for them. "OK, you said you wanted to talk about living arrangements. So, let's talk. I'll do whatever you want, Jess—whatever you're comfortable with," he took a sip of his wine, "as long as it doesn't involve me moving out."

She gulped her wine down. She'd been thinking about this for a while, knowing it was what she wanted. Jesse just hoped it didn't freak him out. "Definitely doesn't involve you moving out—well, not out of the house."

"Ok, go on." AJ quirked his eyebrow at her, waiting for an answer.

"Look... I know the house is a reminder of Alex, but I don't want to leave or move. And I can't see us sleeping apart. Not with you living under the same roof. So," she took another sip of her wine. "I want you to move into my room."

She waited, watching him. He shifted in his chair, placing his napkin down on his plate. "Are you sure? It won't be weird for you to have me in the bedroom you were supposed to share with him?"

"He never made it home to sleep in the house, AJ. Yes, the house was something he and I bought for our future. But he's gone—and I don't want to be alone anymore. If it's too weird for you, I'll move into your room. Don't you understand I want to be with you? Sleep in your arms, wake in your arms, feel you against me?"

AJ inhaled sharply, turning his head towards the back. "Check, please." He called out to the waiter.

"What? Did I upset you?"

"No, Jess, I want to take you home and make love to you. In our room."

She couldn't stifle the nervous giggle that bubbled up. "Well then, let's get out of here."

AJ and Jesse left the restaurant and barely reached the car before AJ pressed her against the passenger door. His lips found hers, kissing her with an intensity that sent heat straight between her legs. She could feel the moisture gather in her panties from his touch, causing her to groan.

"I love you, Jess."

Breaking free of his hold, "I love you too, AJ. Let's go home."

Chapter Fifteen

AJ AND JESSE barely made it into the house. They rushed up the stairs, shedding their clothes as they did. Pushing open her door, Jesse grabbed AJ's hand and led him to the bed.

"It's my turn."

Not giving him the chance to answer, Jesse unbuttoned his pants and shoved them down, taking his underwear down with them. His erection bobbed against his stomach, the tip glistening with pre-cum. Reaching out, Jesse fisted his dick, jerking her palm along the smooth skin as she dropped to her knees.

"Jess, you don't have to do that."

He grabbed her hair, trying to stop her movements, but she leaned forward, taking him in her mouth. Jesse bobbed her head, taking into the depths of her throat.

"Fuck—Jess..."

His moans spurred her on, creating a frenzy of need as she licked and sucked. Jesse palmed his balls, squeezing them slightly, making him jerk out of her mouth.

"Please... Jess, I need to be inside you."

He pulled Jesse up from the floor and slid her sweatshirt over her head. AJ fumbled with the button on Jesse's jeans. Once he had them open, he slipped his palm inside, dipping his fingers into her core. Moaning, Jesse shimmied her hips, eager for him to shove them to her ankles. AJ pushed her to the bed and straddled her body with his. Palming her breast in his hand, AJ sucked her nipple into his mouth.

"Oh, AJ—More, please; I want you inside me."

AJ lined his cock at her opening and eased himself into her wet center. He pushed in and out as her walls swallowed him whole.

"Faster. Fuck, AJ. Please." She begged. His movements became fiercer, making her scream as her release ripped out of her body. He reached between them and flicked his thumb across her swollen nub.

"Come for me, Jess—I want to hear you."

His command was her undoing. Jesse's pussy tightened around his stiff shaft, causing him to grunt. AJ pushed deeper inside as she milked his cock, taking every ounce of his seed inside her. They crumbled to the bed, AJ rolling to his side, pulling Jesse's back against his chest.

"Laying in your arms is better than anything I could imagine."

AJ kissed her neck, snuggling further into against her. Listening to his breath, feeling the warmth as he breathed against her neck, Jesse fell asleep content in his arms.

Jesse woke the next morning with AJ's arms wrapped tightly around her waist. Her head was tucked under his chin, and she felt safe and loved for the first time in a long time. Rolling over, Jesse's eyes caught sight of the folded flag. It didn't make her sad this time. Instead, she felt a sense of relief. Knowing AJ loved her while his brother's memory sat just a short distance away gave her a sense of peace.

"Morning, beautiful." AJ kissed her head.

Jesse ran her hand down his bare chest, her fingers tracing the ridges of his defined muscles. Jesse could feel him stiffen under my touch. "Woman, you do that, and we won't get out of bed."

Jesse giggled, rolling over to straddle him. His hands brushed against her legs, resting firmly on her hips.

"Maybe that's my intention."

She couldn't help herself. Jesse wanted this man so much it hurt. Leaning forward, she pressed her lips against his. His erection pressed into her butt, making her reach around and guide him into her center. The wave of euphoria that consumed her as she rode him was more than she could take. The orgasm burst free from both of them quickly, leaving them a sweaty mess in the bed.

Breathless, Jesse leaned down and kissed him. "I'm going to shower. I guess we need to tear ourselves from this bed and get ready to head over for dinner. I forgot today's Christmas Eve."

"Yep, let's get up." AJ hopped out of bed, smacking her on the butt as he did.

"Race you to the shower!" He took off towards the bathroom.

"Oh, no, you don't. I called it first!"

Giggling, Jesse stumbled in after him, fully aware that they would end up in the shower together. After sharing an intimate moment under the warm water, they emerged dressed and ready for the day.

Discussing plans for dessert, Jesse realized they had forgotten their commitment to Allie.

"I didn't forget; I just had you for dessert last night."

Jesse chuckled, pulling him into a hug.

"Well, I don't think you want to share me with your brother as dessert... so let's run to the store and pick up something before we head over."

"You're right. I'm not sharing you with anyone. So, you best tell your other lady friends you're taken."

"Jess, there's only ever been you."

They got into the car and went to the store, settling on cupcakes before heading to John's. Parking in Jesse's driveway, AJ retrieved the cupcakes from the backseat.

"Ready?" He laced his fingers in Jesse's.

"With you by my side, Jesse is ready for anything."

As they walked into the yard, John pulled in beside them.

"Jess, AJ."

His dad walked towards them, shaking AJ's free hand.

"Hi, Dad. We're glad you came."

Jesse hugged his mom and dad before walking up the steps to Allie's house.

"Thanks for the invite. It's good to be surrounded by family today. This Christmas is going to be hard."

AJ's mom wiped a tear from her cheek. This was the first Christmas they would spend knowing there would be no contact with Alex. They'd spent many holidays without him, but he would always come home. This time, he wouldn't be coming home. It stung to hear his mother admit it out loud, though.

"Jess, we are so glad you're giving AJ a chance. I'm sure you've loved AJ longer, and seeing you both so happy is a true blessing."

His mom changed the subject, smiling as she touched Jesse's shoulder.

"I've loved him just as long—I just loved Alex, too. Now, I can love them both."

Smiling at her, Jesse opened Allie's door, "Allie. John. You guys in here?"

"Yeah. We're in the kitchen! Come on back."

Walking into the kitchen, Jesse found him at the stove.

"Wait, a minute—Allie said she was cooking. Why in the hell are you at the stove?"

He couldn't boil water to save his life. Seeing him standing there stirring something in a pot was an oddity.

"Um... Allie is in the bathroom. I'm just helping her out. And why do you say it like that? I can cook, you know?"

"John, microwave dinners aren't cooking."

He threw the dish towel at Jesse. "Hey now! Allie has taught me to cook. I can make macaroni all on my own."

Laughing, he pulled Jesse into a hug. "I'm glad you're here, sis. AJ, how are you?"

"John," AJ shook his hand, "I'm good. Is there anything I can do to help?"

"Just get my sister off my back—she's giving me crap about my cooking skills."

He winked at Jesse as he turned back to the stove. Allie emerged from the half bathroom, looking deathly pale.

"Allie? God, are you ok?"

"Yeah, great. Oh god…" She took off running back to the bathroom.

"Shit!"

Jesse ran after her, kneeling behind her as she heaved her guts into the toilet.

Pulling her hair back, "Allie—honey, if you're sick, we can cancel dinner."

"No, it's good. I'll be ok in a minute."

"Your wife is being stubborn."

AJ's mom was standing behind Jesse. "We should let her rest. Come on; I can buy everyone dinner out."

"NO—Wait. Please…" Allie pushed Jesse off and stood. "Damn, I had it all planned out. This is not how I wanted to tell everyone."

Allie walked past them, taking her into his arms as she sobbed against him.

Emerging from the bathroom, AJ took Jesse's hand in his. "Allie, what is it? What did you need to tell us?"

She couldn't stop crying. John ran his hand down her hair. "Shhhhh, baby—they won't care how we tell them. Just tell them."

Jesse stared at them, wrapped in each other's arms, fearing the worst. Was Allie sick? She couldn't bear to watch her brother go through something like that. He loved her way too much to lose her.

"Allie, are you sick? Please—just tell me."

She turned her head towards Jesse. "Well, yeah, I'm sick. But not for the reason you think. I, we're..." she took a deep breath. "Jess, you're going to be an aunt. I'm pregnant."

The words echoed through the room, staring at her, then looking at her brother. Jesse realized what she had said.

"What? Pregnant?"

Jesse moved to stand before her and her brother, placing a hand on her belly.

"How long? Are you sure?"

Jesse fired off the questions.

"Yes—about 12 weeks. We didn't want to tell anyone until I knew for sure. I was just barely pregnant when we went out and didn't know. I had to make sure I didn't do something to the baby from all my drinking. But the doctor assured me everything is good. I go for the first ultrasound on Tuesday."

Jesse pulled them into a hug. "Oh, my god! You're going to be a dad—and me an aunt! This is fantastic news!!"

They all hugged them, excited at the prospect of a baby in the family. Even AJ's parents were excited. Besides his in-laws, John had no one else. AJ's mom and dad had become surrogate parents to both of them. So, to them, this was going to be like their first grandchild as well. Maybe this Christmas wouldn't suck after all.

Chapter Sixteen

CHRISTMAS CAME and went with no issues. Allie continued to battle morning sickness, and Jesse couldn't help but feel empathy for her. Despite the challenges, the cause behind it kept a smile on Allie's face. The week following Christmas, she and John visited the doctor and learned that the baby's due date was set for June 12th—a perfect alignment with their summer break.

The timing worked well for Allie. It would be the start of summer vacation when their family's addition arrived. Although concerned about morning sickness affecting her teaching, Jesse reassured her she'd be there to support her.

For Christmas, Jesse gave AJ a new watch, replacing the one destroyed in his car accident. In return, AJ gifted Jesse a crystal heart pendant, symbolizing strength and protection, reminding him of her fragile heart.

On a day when AJ was away for ninja training, Jesse found herself on the couch, having prepared several lesson plans. The end of the Christmas break marked the return to work, and the exhaustion settled in. Despite the fatigue, Jesse reflected on the blessing of time spent with AJ, even though they had almost lost each other.

"Jess, you here?"

"Yeah, in the living room."

John entered, looking visibly tired. His disheveled uniform and weary appearance hinted at his ongoing struggle with sleep.

"Damn, you look like crap."

"Uh, well, I feel like crap. That's why I'm here. I need your help, sis."

"Sure, what is it? I owe you."

"Allie's making me nuts. I love her... I do, but this morning, sickness and her moodiness are making me lose my mind. What do I do?"

"What do you mean?"

"Jess, she's turned into a cranky, crying, hungry, angry, throwing-up monster." He sighed heavily, running his hands through his short hair.

"That's called pregnancy. But I'll help; what can I do?"

"I don't know, take her out... shopping, anything. She is going stir-crazy sitting in the house. It's like she's letting the morning sickness hold her hostage. I'm surprised she's even going to work."

"I'll talk to her. She needs to live normally; a little morning sickness shouldn't keep her from being her. You need to get some rest. Are you working right now?"

"No—kind of... ugh. I told my secretary I was going home to rest and wasn't feeling well. She will call if something major happens."

"Well, go upstairs. Use AJ's old room and get some sleep. I'll go over and drag her out for some girl time. She needs that just as much as you need sleep."

He stood, walking towards Jesse, and kissed her head. "You're the best. Thank you."

Jesse watched him ascend the stairs and, hearing AJ's door shut, walked outside. Pulling out her phone, she sent AJ a text, informing him that John was sleeping and she was taking Allie out for a girl's day. It was Sunday, ensuring a less crowded trip into San Diego.

"Allie?" Jesse called out as she opened their door. "You in here?"

"Yeah—Jess, I'm in the bathroom. Throwing up again."

She walked out, looking defeated.

"Damn, Allie, when did you last shower?"

"Friday—I think..."

"Go shower... I'll wait. We're going shopping. John's at my house asleep, and you need a girl's day out. Morning sickness or not... so no arguments."

Jesse shooed her upstairs, following closely. "You get in the shower. I'll find you some clothes."

"Jess, seriously. I don't want to go out in public and puke."

"Allie, you're not the first pregnant woman to have sickness. And you won't be the last. Now, I need some girl time, you need some girl time, and your husband needs some sleep. So,... No is not an option."

"Fine... But get me some yoga pants. This little butter bean has decided to show, and none of my clothes fit."

"Well then, we need to get you some maternity things! So, see... we have a reason to go out!"

Allie showered quickly and got dressed in yoga pants and a long shirt. Despite not feeling it, she looked radiant. Pregnancy, sickness, and all made her look beautiful.

"So," Allie shifted in her seat as they drove, "how's it going with AJ?"

"Perfect. I can't believe how lucky I am."

Jesse couldn't help but smile as she drove. "He loves me and understands that a part of me will always love Alex. I couldn't ask for a better person to give my heart to again."

"John and I knew that this would happen. We are so glad you gave him a chance. That boy has loved you since high school. If I'm being honest, I was surprised you married his brother."

"Well, fate certainly had other plans in the long run. Enough with the heavy stuff—have you guys thought of any names for the baby?"

"Actually, we have. We want to name it after your dad if it's a boy. And if it's a girl—well, we can't decide... or agree."

"So, Hunter... After my dad?"

"I figured he would want to name his son after our dad, so that didn't surprise me."

"Yeah—you ok with that?"

"Of course! I always assumed John would name his first son after his dad. It's nice, you know—to have his legacy carried on like that. I just wish he were here to meet his grandbaby."

"He does, too. This way, we are making him.

part of his grandkids."

"Why not name the girl after my mom?"

"We figured you'd want that honor."

"Well, I don't see having kids anytime soon—maybe you should just use her name."

"Nah—you'll have kids. Just watch... you and AJ will make cute babies."

Jesse couldn't help but picture her and AJ's kids. They would make some damn fine babies together one day. Allie and Jesse continued to talk as they drove. Once they made it to the mall, they spent the afternoon shopping and talking about the future. It did them some good to get out of the house and spend time together.

When they got home, AJ had already cooked dinner for them. John was well-rested and very thankful that his wife was feeling better. The pregnancy was taking a toll on both of them, but it would be worth it in the long run.

As they left, Jesse turned to AJ. "So, random question... Do you want kids?"

"Humm..." scooping her up, he threw her over his shoulder, "Let's go practice making some right now."

"AJ, you loon, put me down!"

Smacking her butt, "I will once I have you upstairs in that bed of ours."

Jesse loved the sound of him saying 'ours.' The future was looking better as the fragments of her heart slowly knitted back together. AJ made her whole.

Chapter Seventeen

AS JESSE SAT across the lunchroom table, she marveled at how much Allie had changed since Christmas. Valentine's Day had arrived, and Allie appeared to be eight months pregnant.

"Are you excited?" Carmen asked.

"Nervous, excited—all that wrapped into one."

Carmen chuckled, "What are you hoping the sex of the baby will be?"

"I don't care, as long as he or she is healthy. But... I'm sure John's hoping for a boy."

Allie, rubbing her protruding baby bump, exuded joy. The couple had an appointment later that day to determine the baby's sex.

"Well, I don't care either. I'm just excited to be an aunt."

"You got any plans for Valentine's Day, Carmen?"

"Nope—this being single sucks on V-Day. What about you?"

135

"AJ has something planned but won't tell me what."

"That's right! I almost forgot he has some surprise planned for you. Any guesses what it is?"

"Nope. He just said wear a dress."

"I bet he's going to propose," Carmen suggested with a smile.

"Wait, you think so?"

"You never know. He has loved you for... I don't know, forever." She laughed as she headed towards her classroom.

"Allie, do you think that's his surprise? Oh. My. God."

"Jess, so what if it is? You and he are good together. You've helped him, and he has helped you. Besides—you deserve this second chance. Don't screw it up out of fear."

"Yeah. I guess so."

Jesse walked to her classroom, her mind racing with thoughts of AJ. The day sped by, and she rushed out of the school at the last bell, needing to get home and change. AJ was adamant about her being ready for their date by 5:30.

After a quick shower, she slipped on a new pair of silky panties and a matching bra. Pulling on the red dress she had bought for the occasion, she admired herself in the mirror. Having put back on some weight, her fuller breasts complemented the dress perfectly. Confident AJ would be pleased with her appearance, she went downstairs to wait for him.

Coming from the base, AJ had assured her he was already dressed. She heard the door shut to his jeep—a new one replacing the totaled vehicle from his accident. This one was black and jacked up.

Letting out a long whistle, Jesse remarked, "Damn Jesse, we may not make it out of the house with you looking like that." His eyes roamed the entire length of her body. Licking his lips, he pulled her close, pressing his mouth to hers. His tongue slipped between her lips, eliciting a soft moan.

"No way—you have to wait. I went all out to look good for you."

"You could wear a burlap sack, and I would find you sexy."

Giving him one last kiss, she pulled away from his grasp. "Let's go. I. AM. STARVED."

Hand in hand, they walked from the house together. AJ opened the passenger door, helping her hoist herself into the jeep.

"Alright—you ready? I have dinner reservations for us at Bently's."

Bently's, an upscale steak restaurant in San Diego, typically took weeks to get a reservation.

"Wow, I'm impressed. Doesn't it take weeks to get a reservation?"

"Good thing I made them four weeks ago."

Smirking, he backed out of the driveway. Jesse grabbed his hand and kissed his knuckles.

"Glad you did. This will be a fantastic night."

"Baby—dinner is just the beginning."

They arrived at the restaurant and were seated almost immediately. AJ ordered for both of them, impressing Jesse even more.

"So, AJ. You never really answered me the other day. Do you want kids?"

"Yes—a couple. What about you?"

"Same... a couple. I am so excited to find out what Allie is having. What do you think it'll be? Boy or Girl?"

"Both."

"Both? You think so?"

"Yeah, look how big she is already. I bet it's twins."

Jesse sat, thinking about his prediction. He was right—Allie was huge to be so early in her pregnancy.

"You may be right—she is huge."

They finished dessert and the bottle of wine. AJ paid the bill and stood. Holding out his hand, "You ready for your surprise?"

Taking his hand, Jesse replied, "Yes... you have me intrigued."

Together, they walked outside towards the boardwalk. It was not that chilly out, so walking felt great.

"Where are we going?"

"To the boardwalk. That, ok?"

"That's perfect. The sun is setting, so it'll be a beautiful view."

They walked, Jesse nestled against his side, to the end of the pier. The view was breathtaking—the sun setting below the coastline, giving the waters a ruby tint.

"This is beautiful. AJ, this is the perfect ending to a perfect night."

Turning to kiss her, Jesse found him on one knee. Her breath hitched as she stepped backward.

"Jesse, I know things happened that were awful. We both lost someone we loved. But through the darkness, you made room for me in your heart. I've loved you since we were kids. I love you now, and I'll love you forever. I thought the hardest thing I would do in life would be watching you from a distance while my brother loved you. But I was wrong. The hardest thing I did was watching you almost die from a broken heart. Fate stepped in and gave me the chance to heal your fragile heart after Alex died."

Shifting on his knees, he pulled a small blue box from his pocket. "Jess, I can't imagine a life where you're not in it. I know the road that led me here was not what we would have chosen for ourselves. But it is one we've traveled together. Please do me the honor and allow me to love you for eternity. Say you'll marry me."

He opened the box, displaying the beautiful diamond ring inside. Jesse stood stunned, staring at the glittering stone. Finally, releasing the breath she didn't realize she was holding, she dropped to her knees in front of AJ.

"Yes... Yes, AJ." Jess's tears spilled down her cheeks as AJ pulled her into his arms, kissing her hard. His hands went into her hair, pulling her hard against his body. Jess whispered against his hold. "AJ, take me home."

Pulling her up to stand with him, he kissed her again. "I love you, Jess. You're all I've wanted, and now that I have you—I want to show you how much you will be treasured for eternity."

"Start with taking me home and making love to me."

They hurried back to the car, sneaking kisses as they went. The hour drive was torturous, as they couldn't keep their hands off each other. They barely entered the house before AJ had her in his arms again. Hoisting her into the air, she wrapped her legs around him as he carried her upstairs.

Pressing her into the bed, he sat back, admiring her laid out before him. "Damn, you're beautiful."

Pushing him back with her feet, she shimmied off the bed and unzipped her dress, letting it fall to the floor. AJ sucked in a breath, confirming he liked what he saw.

"You like?"

"Like? LOVE is more like it. You look amazing."

He ran his hands across the silky panties as he pulled her flush against him. She could feel how much he liked what he saw, excitement bubbling in her chest. He pressed her into the bed, taking his time to explore her body. He reached behind her, unfastening her bra, letting it fall onto the bed. Cupping her breast in his hand, he ran his thumb across her nipple. His touch was electric, causing her to suck in a breath.

He slowly kissed his way down her body. Slipping the silky panties down her legs, he buried his face in her center. Licking and biting at her clit. As he sucked, he slipped on a finger—pleasuring her with his mouth and hand. Unable to control herself, she pulled him towards her, catching his mouth on hers. Pushing him to his back, she lowered herself even with his cock. It was standing at attention, begging for her touch. She swirled her tongue around the base before taking him in her mouth fully.

"Jess—god, you feel so good," grabbing her shoulders, "Wait, I have an idea."

He pulled her to him, gripping her hips as he spun her around so that she was straddling him backward. Pushing her back, he urged her to bend over. Leaning forward, she took him in her mouth once again, only to feel him slip a finger inside her. She moaned against him, feeling his cock twitch against her cheek. She felt him tug her towards him until she sat on his face. He dipped his warm tongue into her folds, lapping up her juices as she swallowed his cock deeper still.

She couldn't suppress the moans coming out of her. The heat between them was nearly unbearable. "AJ—God, I need to have you inside me NOW." She spun, grabbing him as she speared herself on him.

"Ahhhh... Jess." AJ moaned as she moved. Leaning back, her hair falling to her back as she rode him. Their rhythm was needy and demanding. He thrust his hips, urging her faster. Grabbing her, he flipped her over. "I want to look into your eyes when you come."

He rammed into her, pressing himself deeper than she thought possible. Kissing her, his hand found its way to her center. Rubbing her sensitive nub, she could feel the climax building.

"OH GOD—I'm so close...Please, AJ, don't stop."

"That's it, baby. Let go."

He slammed into her, pulling almost out and slamming into her again. Pinching her clit. Her center squeezed around him, pulling out the screams of ecstasy. Together, they fell over the edge of the desire—their juices mixing as they came. Spent from the lovemaking, they fell asleep holding one another. His warm body felt so right pressed against her.

She couldn't imagine being anywhere else.

Chapter Eighteen

TWO YEARS HAD PASSED since Alex's death. Jesse still hurt from his loss, but AJ had given her something she could never have found on her own—love. She sat at the lunch table with friends, listening to them talk about the summer break, which was not nearly close enough. Allie was due in less than two months, carrying twins, and doctors were concerned about a premature delivery.

Yep, AJ was right. Allie and John were having twin boys, and Jess was ecstatic about becoming an aunt. The decision to get married had been made, with an October wedding planned to allow Allie enough time to recover from giving birth during the summer.

"So, Allie—how are you feeling?" Carmen asked, waiting for a response.

"Like a frigging whale, that's how. I am so happy, but I can't wait for these two boys to get out. It feels like two boxers are inside my gut. I swear they don't stop moving," Allie said, placing her hand on the swell of her belly. "What about you, Jess? You excited about your upcoming wedding?"

"It seems so surreal to me. Part of me is so happy I can't stand it. But then, especially today, I feel guilty. You know…"

Today marked the second anniversary of Alex's funeral. Jesse felt pressure in her chest just thinking about him, making her breath catch.

"Whoa—Jess… Take a breath, babe," Carmen said, touching her back. "You're giving yourself a panic attack. Jess, it's okay. We know today is hard for you. But Alex would be happy for you—you know that."

Her words rang in Jesse's ears. She knew moving on was what Alex would want for her, but some of her would always feel like she was betraying him. "Yeah, I know." She took a deep breath, calming herself the best she could. Shaking off the impending panic attack, Jess turned to Allie and changed the subject. "So, did you guys think of another name? Hunter needs a name for his brother."

"Well—yeah, but I wanted to talk with you first. But it can wait."

Jesse furrowed her brows. "Why me?"

"Jess, I think we should wait. We can talk about it tomorrow at home. You nearly had a panic attack. The last thing I want to do is send you in one for real." Allie smiled, although Jess could tell it was forced.

"Allie, what is it you need to talk about? You're freaking me out." Jesse urged her to spit it out.

"Fine. I'll just ask you. John and I have been talking, and we wanted to name the other baby Alexander."

Jesse sat, stunned, running Allie's words through her mind. She didn't want to sound like a bitch, but them naming the baby Alexander was not their right. It was hers and AJ's.

"Look, if it's too weird, we won't do it. But we thought carrying on his name like that would be nice. Tell me what you're thinking... Please?"

"I... What if AJ wants to name our kid after his brother?" Jesse snapped.

"Oh, damn... I hadn't thought about that. You're right—never mind. I'm sorry, Jess, I didn't consider that possibility." Allie reached across and squeezed Jess's hand.

"No, it's okay. But I think we should leave that name for AJ if he wants it."

They finished their lunch and stood to leave the cafeteria. As the three of them stood, a wave of nausea hit Jesse. Carmen grabbed her by the arm. "Jess—you, ok? You look awfully pale."

"I don't know, I don't feel good all of a sudden. My lunch isn't settling right. I'm going to run to the bathroom. Can you watch my class for me?"

Carmen tipped her head and shrugged. "Sure. I got them."

Allie bit down on her lip, "Jess, I hope I didn't upset you by asking about the name."

"Nah, Allie. I just feel queasy suddenly. It's not because of that, I promise. We're good."

Nausea hit again. Pushing away from the table, Jesse bolted to the bathroom, barely making it in before throwing up her lunch. Sweating and dizzy, she stepped out of the stall, grabbed the sink's edge, and turned on the water. She suddenly felt like crap.

Her phone vibrated in their pocket. Retrieving it, she noticed a text from AJ.

AJ: You alright? Allie texted and said you were sick.

Me: Yeah—I think. Maybe something I ate.

AJ: Can you go home and rest?

Me: Going to talk to administration now. Will let you know.

AJ: K—love you. Let me know what I can do.

Me: Love you too.

Jesse shoved her phone back into her pocket. Jesse gathered herself by splashing water on her face before walking out of the bathroom and heading to the office. The principal took one look at her and told her to leave. After farming out her last two classes, she headed to her car.

Barely making it to the parking lot, Jesse threw up next to her car in the grass. How she made it home without vomiting again, Jesse wasn't sure. As soon as she pulled into the drive-way, she dry-heaved into the front yard. Once she made it inside, she texted AJ, letting him know she was home and going straight to bed. Stumbling upstairs, Jesse pushed through the door and collapsed on the bed. This was the worst she'd felt in a long time.

Jesse woke to the doorbell ringing. Shaking from the sleep haze, Jesse slowly stood from the bed. Grabbing her phone from her pocket, where it was still tucked, she noticed twenty-six missed calls and a slew of text messages.

Everyone had been trying to call her.

The doorbell rang again, reminding Jesse of what had woken her up. Shaking her head, Jesse started down the steps, swiping her phone to call John, her brother, back. He'd been half of the missed calls, and part of her worried something was wrong with Allie. Entranced with the screen of her phone, she didn't notice who was at her door when she jerked it open.

"Yeah—can I..." dropping her phone to the floor when she looked up to meet the eyes of two uniformed Navy men standing before them.

The world went black as she crumpled to the ground, vaguely hearing them say her name. "Ms. Holt?"

Coming out of their darkness, Jesse could hear someone talking as she slowly opened her eyes. "She fainted, Mr. Holt."

"I told you to wait for me." AJ's pissed-off voice penetrated the fog as the room came into view. "Jess—Jesus, are you okay?"

AJ kneeled in front of her. "AJ." She shifted to sit up. Looking around the room, she spotted the two uniformed military men standing against the wall. "Wait, what happened? Why are they here?"

AJ wiped a piece of their hair from their face. "Jess—something has happened."

Jesse watched as his eyes brimmed with tears. Cupping his cheek, "AJ—what? God... when I saw them standing there, I thought they were here to tell me you were dead. I guess I fainted."

He pulled Jesse into his arms. "Baby—I'm fine. But there's something I need to tell you. Ok?"

She leaned back and stared into his eyes. "AJ, you're scaring me. Please, what's happened?" John burst through the door, and Allie and AJ's parents walked in behind him. Jesse glanced at them, then back at Jesse. "Wait, what the hell is going on? Why is everyone here—AJ? What happened?"

"Jess, It's about Alex."

Jesse's face scrunched in confusion. "Alex?"

She could see the torment in AJ's eyes as he spoke. "Jess—Alex..."

He shook his head, tears falling down his cheeks as he searched for his words. Words Jesse never thought she'd hear. Words she wasn't ready for.

"They found him alive, Jess. He's not dead.

The world ceased its motion, and her breath caught in her throat. Surely, she had misheard him.

"What? What do you mean, AJ—what are you saying?"

AJ's voice was filled with hope as he spoke. "Jess. He didn't die. He's been a prisoner for the last two years. Do you hear what I'm saying, Jess? Alex is alive."

His mother crumpled to the floor, his dad grabbing her and holding her tight. Her sobs echoed through the living room. Jesse absorbed the news, but the shock still coursed through her body. She had to see him with her own eyes to believe anything she was being told. "Where is he?"

"Ma'am, he's being transported to the base in San Diego from Germany today." One of the Navy officers spoke from where he stood, watching the scene unfold.

Standing, she turned to Don, AJ, and Alex's dad. "Is this real, Dad?"

"Yes, darling—Alex is alive."

Crumpling to her knees, AJ kneeled beside her. "Jesse, he's alive."

Pulling her into his arms, she let the tears fall. Alex, her Alex, was alive—not dead. A wave of nausea hit her hard. "Oh god —I'm going to be sick." She pushed up off the floor, running to the bathroom, barely making it before she threw up. Vomiting between her sobs, she felt AJ's hands on her shoulders.

"Jess, baby—are you ok? What can I do?"

Wiping her face, she stood and turned towards AJ. "Take me to him. I need to see him. Please, AJ." AJ nodded his head and took her hand. His thumb ran across her engagement ring, his eyes brimming with tears. "AJ. This doesn't change anything."

"Jess. It changes everything. But now's not the time to talk about this. Let's get to the base and see what they can tell us." They walked out of the bathroom, hand in hand. "Ok—tell me what you know," AJ addressed the uniformed officer in the living room.

"Yes, Sir. As you know, we received information that he was alive and being held hostage, along with another marine. Special Ops went in and retrieved the two captives. The Commander on base has more details. We can take you there now if you like. His plane is due to arrive at nine tonight."

Looking at the clock, she realized it was six. She had slept for almost four hours. Nodding at them, she turned to AJ. "Let's go. I want to see what more they can tell us. Do you know if he is talking—or how he is physically?"

"No, ma'am. We don't have those details. We were just instructed to come and notify the next of kin. With you being his wife, we came here first."

She looked down at the engagement ring on her finger. "Wife." She looked up at AJ. "Oh my god, I'm still married."

"No, Jess—you're not. You're a widow."

Her brother came to stand beside her. "Jess, look at me. You are not married. It's been two years. Stop worrying about this. You're engaged to AJ now. This is just—Fuck, I don't know what this is."

John turned to look at Don. "He's right, Jess. In the eyes of the law, you are no longer married—so let go of the guilt. I can see it all over your face right now."

AJ pulled her tighter. "Jess—we will work this all out. No matter what, I love you, ok?"

"Ok." But inside, she was fighting a battle. She loved AJ, and the thought of losing him tore at her fiber. But the other half of her was overjoyed that Alex was alive.

"Jess—you don't look good."

"Yeah, I still feel terrible. But let's go. I want to get to the base." Turning toward AJ's parents, "Meet you guys there?" His parents nodded and walked out the door.

John grabbed her arm and tugged her into a hug. "Jess, Allie, and I will meet you there. I love you, Kiddo."

She gave him a half smile and pulled free of his grasp. "Love you too."

The hour it took to get there felt like an eternity. AJ and she sat in silence with their thoughts. Now and then, she glanced at him, watching his tense expression play on his face. She knew he felt the same mixture of emotions as she did. He was worried about them, concerned about her, and most of all, worried about his brother.

Being held prisoner did things to a man's soul. Would Alex even be the same person he was before? This was one of her many questions; instead, she needed answers.

"AJ—pull over." Jesse gripped the door handle as AJ abruptly pulled over onto the shoulder and slammed the brakes. Jesse threw open her door in time to vomit. AJ rubbed her back, holding her hair from her face.

"Jess, maybe you should see a doctor."

"No—I'm fine. It's just something I ate, and with all this excitement and stress... well, it's not helping matters."

Slowly, he pulled back onto the roadway. As they pulled onto the base, her anxiety level rose exponentially. "Take it easy, Jess. I'm here with you every step of the way."

She squeezed his hand, nodding as the tears slipped down her face. Still in a state of shock, they pulled into a parking place. AJ was at her door before she could get out. "Here, let me help you."

Standing, she wobbled on her feet. Leaning into AJ for support, they walked into headquarters. They were greeted by LT. Commander Wynn. "AJ, Mrs. Holt. Come with me to the briefing area. Your family is already in there waiting." He led them down a narrow corridor and into a small sitting room.

Don and Betty sat at the small round table, and John sat on the sofa beside Allie. "Ok, have a seat." he motioned to the empty chairs. "Here is what we know. Alex was held captive just outside of Qatar, close to where his chopper went down. I will not lie to you. He is beat up. They broke his hand... among other things."

The tears rolled down her face as she there sat speechless. Alex was alive. This was happening.

"His mental state is questionable, and it appears he is suffering from some memory loss. We don't know how much or how little he remembers. He will be taken to the medical facility for evaluation and recovery when he arrives here. It will be a while before we can let you see him."

"I'll wait."

"Mrs. Holt, I just want you to prepare yourself. He is not the Alex you remember. It is likely he is suffering from PTSD and will have outbursts. I need to think of your safety as well. Ok?"

AJ scrubbed his hand down his face as he spoke. "Commander, has he said anything about his family? Anything at all?" The lines of worry appeared as he questioned the commander.

"No, AJ, I'm afraid he hasn't. Look, this will be rough for the next couple of days. I have set up one of the empty quarters for you to use. You should go there and try to rest. He won't be here for a couple of hours—and even then, it will be several more before you can see him."

Nodding, AJ and she stood. "Ok. Thanks, Commander Holt."

"Please, call me Jack. And if you need anything, let one of the support members know. They will get it for you or find me." Turning to a uniformed officer, "Show them to the rooms."

They were guided down a hallway towards some empty sleeping quarters. AJ's parents took the first room. Allie and John were next, leaving the last room for AJ and her.

Walking in, she took a deep breath, letting a sob escape her chest.

"Jess, please, baby. It will be ok. I promise you," turning her to face him, "I love you, baby. We will figure everything out." He wiped his thumb across her cheek, catching the lone tear drifting from her eye.

"I'm so scared, AJ. I don't want to lose you—I... I know that's selfish because Alex is alive."

Pulling her against his chest, "You aren't going to lose me. I promise."

Slowly, AJ set her down on the bed. He removed her shoes, slipping her feet under the covers. Moving around the side of the bed, he crawled into the bed with her. Pulling her close to his body, they lay like this for a while before finally giving in to sleep.

The soft tapping at the door woke her from her restless sleep. "Mrs. Holt, Mr. Holt? Commander requested you in the briefing room."

"Ok, thanks," she shimmied out of AJ's hold. "AJ, wake up. They need us."

AJ stretched, standing beside the bed. "Here." he dug in his pocket, pulling out some gum. "No toothbrush. Figured this would help."

"Are you telling me I have bad breath?"

Pulling her flush against his chest, he kissed her. "I couldn't care less what your breath smells like… But I know you, and you will worry when we go out there to talk with everyone."

He was right. She would be paranoid. And they didn't pack an overnight bag in their rush to get to the base. "Thanks." She smiled as she took his hand. "You ready?"

"Question is, are you ready?"

A nervous chuckle escaped Jesse's chest. "Nope…"

They walked down the hallway, greeted by everyone in the briefing room. "OK—Alex arrived last night at about nine-thirty. He's been moved into the medical ward. Jess, he asked for you."

It was like a boulder hit her in the gut. Alex remembered her and even asked for her. She looked at AJ and could see the worry in his eyes. It looked like he thought this was the end. "Ok, take me to see him."

"Let me warn you. He isn't as bad as reported, though he has some bruises and cuts. Other than his hand, he's the Alex we remember." Commander Holt reiterated that Alex was a changed man.

"Fine—let's just go, ok?" Jesse glanced around at the faces watching her. It was like they were waiting for her to lose her shit.

"Follow me."

AJ held her hand as they followed the commander through several hallways. They entered the medical ward and were greeted by a dozen stares. Each head followed her as they stopped just outside his door. "Mrs. Holt, are you ready to go in?"

She turned to AJ. "I need to do this alone."

AJ nodded, releasing her hand as he backed away. She grabbed his hand, tugging him into a hug. "I love you, AJ—that doesn't change..." kissing him before she released him.

"I love you too, Jess. I'm right outside for you."

She took a deep breath as the commander opened the door to his room.

<h1 style="text-align:center;">*Chapter Nineteen*</h1>

"JESSE."

Hearing his voice startled her. She stared at the man on the bed—the man who was supposed to be her dead husband. She couldn't move.

"I'll leave you two to talk. Jess, I'll be right outside. Come get me when you're done." Nodding, unable to speak, she watched as the commander shut the door, leaving her in the room alone with Alex.

"Jesse," Alex spoke in a raspy voice.

She couldn't speak. He looked just like the Alex she remembered. Just thinner. "Alex." Her voice was barely audible. Frozen to her spot, she stared at the man she once loved.

He patted the bed. "Come sit. Please."

Walking towards him, she slid into the chair beside his bedside and sat down. She couldn't bring herself to sit so close—not yet. It was too much to take in. "Alex—I... you died. I buried you."

The tears streamed down her cheeks, pooling on her shirt. He reached out and ran his thumb across her tear-stained cheek. "I'm so sorry. I tried to get back to you—I swear."

Fiddling with her hands in her lap, she looked down at her entwined fingers. What was she supposed to do? She buried him—moved on, and was getting married to his brother, of all people. "Alex. I—I don't know what to say. This is all so overwhelming."

"It's ok. We will get through this. I never stopped loving you, Jess. You're the reason I survived the last two years."

Guilt plagued her—It felt like someone sliced her heart in two. She loved Alex, just not in the same way anymore. Smiling at him, "Let's just get you better, ok?"

A soft knock at the door as it opened revealed his parents and AJ. "Alex!" his mother rushed to his side, sobbing as she embraced him.

"Mom, it's ok...I'm home now."

She turned, smiling at AJ as he walked over to his brother. "Alex... God, I can't believe this!"

He ran to his bedside, hugging him as best he could. Alex patted him on the back. "AJ—glad you came. I'm sorry I put everyone through this."

"Alex—don't blame yourself. We are just so damn happy you're alive."

She sat, watching the two brothers interact. Confusion ran through her blood. She knew beyond any doubt she loved AJ heart and soul. But she felt like she was supposed to love Alex —after all, she'd loved him once. She watched as everyone said hello. John and Allie had come into the room.

"Wow, Allie—you're huge."

"Alex!" his mother yelled.

Allie patted her protruding mound. "No, it's ok. I am huge. Yep. Carrying twins. I'm due in two months... if I make it that long."

"Sorry—I didn't mean to sound so rude. You look radiant. Congratulations. Jess,"

Alex reached for her, shoving her left hand in her pocket to hide the ring she forgot to remove. She took his hand in hers. "Alex, there is so much to talk about—to tell you. But you need your rest. We will come back in a couple of hours, ok?"

"Ok... Jess, can't you stay with me?"

She looked at AJ, pleading for his help silently, "Alex, Doc said you needed your rest—don't worry, we'll be back later."

"Fine..." Alex tugged her until she stumbled, falling onto his bed.

"Ale-" He silenced her with a kiss.

She quickly pulled away from him, shocked at his display of affection. But Alex just grinned like it was the normal thing to do. "Sorry—I dreamed of that for the last two years."

"It's fine." She brushed her shirt down, turning away from him. Taking in AJ's expression, she could tell he was feeling conflicted. It pained her to see him hurting. She smiled at him, hoping he could see into her soul—knowing she was his. "I'll be back later."

"Jess." she turned back to face Alex when he called her name. "I love you—you kept me alive."

Forcing a half smile, she left the room. Walking halfway down the corridor, she propped herself against the wall—sliding down to the floor. Her sobs echoed through the empty hallway.

"Jess. Baby," AJ kneeled in front of her.

"AJ, what am I going to do? You heard him—I kept him alive all this time. I... this is going to crush him."

AJ stood, scooped her off the floor, and cradled her to his chest. He carried her back to their sleeping quarters. "Jess—what do you want to do? I won't lie to you. It will kill me if you go back to him. But I get it—you were his wife. I love you too much to hold you back from your second chance at love."

Reaching up, she cupped his face in her hand. "AJ, you are my second chance. I love you—and seeing him in the flesh confirmed it... I love him, but I am not in love with him anymore. My heart will always hold a spot for him, but I've moved on. You're who I love."

"Of course, you feel that way now. But once you've had time to spend with him... Jess, he had your heart first."

Jesse shook her head back and forth, his words cutting her like fire. "Can we just not talk about this—not now? Please, AJ... hold me."

"As much as I would love to hold you, you must eat. You still look pale, and I can't remember the last time you put food in your stomach. So, let's grab some food from the mess hall. Then we can come back here, and I will hold you as long as you want."

She looked at her ring, smiling. She nodded. "You take such good care of me, AJ—this isn't fair to you."

"Jess. I'd walk through fire for you."

They walked into the nearly empty mess hall. It was almost ten in the morning, so most everyone had already come through and eaten. "Let's get you some food."

AJ led her over to the buffet-style line, handing her a tray. "Get whatever you want."

Smiling, she piled eggs, pancakes and some bacon on her plate. AJ cut his eyes at her and then at her plate.

"I guess I was hungrier than I thought."

Grinning, he led them to an empty table after paying for their breakfast. She scarfed down her food, barely leaving any time to taste the flavors.

"Damn woman—you were hungry."

"Shut up... being sick left a lot of space in my stomach."

He smiled as he shoveled another forkful of pancakes into his mouth. After he finished, they stood, taking their plates to the trashcan. She was overcome with a wave of dizziness as they walked towards the door. AJ grabbed her to steady her on her feet.

"Christ Jess—you, ok?"

"I don't know. I just got dizzy. Maybe I should see a doctor. I'd hate to get Alex sick when he's trying to heal."

"You can go see the base doctor. Come on, I'll walk you over there." They headed out of the mess hall and walked towards the medical wing. "Cassie," AJ called out to a young nurse standing at the desk, "Any chance a doctor could check out Jess? She's been having dizzy spells and vomiting. I'm sure it's just all the stress, with Alex returning from the dead."

The nurse looked shocked. "What? Alex is alive? Oh my God."

"Yeah, he's on the second floor. You should go see him later. But right now, I need to know that she's," he pointed to her, "ok."

"Oh, sorry. Yeah, I can get one of the docs to look her over. Can you wait over there a few minutes?"

"Sure, no problem. AJ," turning to face him, "Why don't you go visit with Alex for a while? I can take care of this, then come meet you upstairs."

AJ looked torn. "You sure? I don't mind waiting with you. I want to make sure you're alright."

"We're in a hospital. Seriously. Go. I'm sure you're right, and it's stress combined with eating something bad."

He leaned in and kissed her. "Well, if something changes, have them call me. Promise?"

"Yeah, yeah... now go—see your brother."

She watched him walk off, admiring his backside.

"Eh, excuse me?"

"Oh, sorry," she blushed as she turned to find Cassie staring at her.

"Dr. Maburn can see you. Follow me." Following the nurse into a room, she stumbled into her as she was riddled with another dizzy spell.

"Damn, sorry."

Cassie grabbed her arm, steadying her. "Wow, you don't look so great. Let me check your blood pressure. Sit down right here." She guided her to the chair and pushed up her sleeve.

She sat silently as the nurse checked her vitals. Shaking her head, "Well, your vitals are all normal. Any other symptoms besides the dizziness? Like peeing more frequently or cramping?"

"No cramping, but now that you mention it, I have been peeing more."

"Let's get a urine sample. The doctor will want to rule out a bladder or kidney infection. Go through that door and use a cup on the back of the toilet. Put it in the little window and come back in here. The doctor will be in shortly."

"Thanks for squeezing me in today."

"No problem, besides—this place would do anything for the Holt boys. They're pretty big deals around here." Her eyes twinkled as she spoke.

Jesse smiled at Cassie. "Oh, really. Well, Alex was my husband before he died... And AJ, well, we are engaged now."

Cassie's eyes widened with surprise. "Let me get this straight. You're saying you are engaged to AJ but married to Alex?"

"Was married to Alex. Legally, I am still considered his widow —or something like that."

"Damn, girl. You hit the hottie jackpot to have scored both Holt boys. Maybe you're the legend, not them."

She walked out, leaving her standing in front of the bathroom. After leaving her sample in the window, she sat in the room, waiting for the doctor.

"Mrs. Holt?" An attractive older woman came into the room.

Standing, she stuck her hand out to shake hers. "Nice to meet you. Thanks for seeing me quickly."

"Ah, it's no problem. The Holt brothers are well-liked and respected. And with Alex's surprising return... well, we'd do anything for them." She smiled, motioning for her to sit down. Closing the door, she turned to face her again. "Alright, let's talk. First, let me ask you some questions. Are you currently in a monogamous relationship?"

"I'm sorry. What does that have to do with me being sick? But yes, I am engaged to AJ."

"Well, that answers my curiosity. Sorry. I knew you were married to Alex, so knowing why you're sick perplexed me. Seeing as he has been gone for two years."

"Yes—AJ and I started seeing each other a year ago. But that's none of your business. Just tell me why I'm feeling so dizzy. Or is my personal life more important to you?"

"I'm sorry Jesse... it was rude of me. I just assumed you were still single. And no, your personal life isn't important to me. But your health is. Jess, you're pregnant."

"I'm pregnant... Wait—pregnant?"

She sat, stunned to silence. Of course, AJ and she were intimate—a lot. And they had used nothing since she was on the pill.

"Wait. How's this possible? I'm on the pill."

"The pill isn't foolproof, Jesse. I assume the baby is AJ's?"

"Of course, it's AJ's... Oh God, what am I going to tell Alex?" Jesse buried her face in her hands.

"What do you mean?"

She glanced up at the doctor. "I haven't even told him AJ and I are engaged. He was so happy to see me... he even told me I was why he survived the last two years."

She put her head in her hands again and let the tears spill down her face. "Jesse, you've done nothing wrong. You moved on with your life because you thought he was dead. Now you have a beautiful life growing inside of you."

"Doctor, please don't tell anyone."

Looking into her eyes, she could see her confusion. "Jess, do you want the baby?"

"Yes, of course. I need time to figure out how to tell everyone—Alex especially. He's so fragile right now. I think I need to tell him about AJ and me first. That's going to be enough of a shock for him."

"Well, you need to take care of yourself. I want you to start prenatal vitamins today. It's imperative that you eat and get rest. You have a baby in your belly to think about."

"How far along do you think I am?"

"Well, lay down over here—we will do an ultrasound. If I can't find the baby with this, we will do a transvaginal ultrasound. But let's try this on first. If you're far enough along, we will see him or her on the screen."

Laying back on the table, she pushed her shirt up. Unbuttoning and folding her pants down, she squirted a warm gel on her abdomen. Turning on the screen, she pressed the wand against her belly.

Thump, thump, thump, thump filled the room. The steady drumming of a tiny heartbeat played through the speakers.

"Well, a heartbeat is a significant sign. Let's see if I can find the little booger."

She pressed the wand into her abdomen harder, searching for the culprit of the steady drumming in the room. "Well, I'll be. Look at that."

She turned the screen towards her. "Well, Mrs. Holt... It looks like you have a baby in there. See the sack? By the size of this little peanut, I'd say you're about eight weeks along."

"Eight weeks?"

"Yep—eight weeks, give or take. That would mean your due date will be sometime around," she pulled out a card from her pocket, "October this year."

"Ok."

She was stunned. She was pregnant with AJ's baby, due to marry him in a few months, and her dead husband was not dead.

"Would you like a printout of the ultrasound?"

"Yes, please."

She handed her the image of her baby. She held it tight as she gave her the rundown of when to take the prenatal vitamins. She had given her a sample to take with her, as well as a few numbers of OBs in her town.

"Thanks again, doctor."

"Jesse, I know this is a shock to you... but everything happens for a reason. So, don't fret—everything will work out."

Shaking her hand, she stepped into the elevator, pressing the button for the second floor. Tucking the picture into her pocket, she folded the bag shut. She wasn't ready to tell anyone yet. There were more important things to deal with right now.

Chapter Twenty

STEPPING OFF THE ELEVATOR, Jesse took a deep breath before entering Alex's room. Walking in, she found AJ, his parents, and the doctor in deep conversation.

"Look, Alex has suffered severe head trauma. It's not uncommon for there to be gaps in his memory."

Everyone turned to look at her as she stepped inside and closed the door.

"Jess," AJ rushed to her, grabbing her hand, "what did the doctor say?"

"It's all good. I'm just dehydrated from being sick. No big deal."

"What's in the bag?" AJ reached out to take it from her.

Snatching it from his grasp, he said, "Nothing, just some vitamins to replenish what I lost when I was throwing up."

She looked over to see his mom watching her with curiosity.

AJ simply shrugged. "Well, as long as you're ok."

"Jess? Are you sick?" Alex was awake and was staring at her and AJ's entwined hands.

Pulling it free, "Nah, nothing big. I just had a little stomach bug and was dehydrated. Had a few dizzy spells. What about you?"

"Apparently, I've lost parts of my life—my memory is fucked up."

"Alex, watch your mouth."

Alex grunted. "Sorry, Mom."

"What do you mean, you're missing pieces?" Jesse narrowed her eyes at him.

"Well, I don't remember much about my captivity. And then there are gaps of time before that. I don't even know how long I was gone."

Jesse stiffened. "Two years, Alex. You were gone two years."

"WOW—really?" He looked at his dad for confirmation.

"Yes, son, you were gone that long."

"Jess, surely you didn't wait on me all this time." The room fell silent, and all eyes were on her, waiting on bated breath for her response.

"Alex, let's not talk about that right now. It's not important. Getting you well is."

The sound of AJ's sharp intake of breath cut into her soul. Her words had hurt him, even though she hadn't meant them to. Alex eyed his brother with suspicion. "AJ—please tell me she didn't wait. I couldn't live with myself."

AJ took a deep breath. "Alex, that's not important right now."

"What the heck—I need to know, Jess, AJ."

AJ retook her hand. "Jess, it's ok. Tell him."

Alex looked between AJ and her, taking in his closeness to her. "Alex, you were dead. For a year, I was barely surviving. Then I got your letter—do you remember the one you wrote? You said you didn't want me to live a life waiting for you. That you needed me to be happy."

"Jess—please don't cry. I'm not mad... I just need to know if there's a chance for us."

"I can't..." She pulled free from AJ's hand and ran from the room.

Rushing out into the hallway, she leaned against the wall. Her breath came in fast, hyperventilating, as his words played over in her mind.

"Jess." Betty had come out to check on her.

"What have I done?"

"Oh, honey, no one could have seen this coming. You did what anyone would do in your place. You fell in love again and learned to live after your heart was shattered. I know this is hard, but Alex will understand."

"Will he? I fell in love with his brother. How can he possibly forgive me?"

Sobbing as Betty pulled her into her arms. "If he doesn't forgive you, then he never truly loved you."

"I'm so confused. I love AJ. I do. But that's Alex sitting in there. He was the man who stole my heart. I need to go. Can I borrow your car? I just need some time away from all this. Tell AJ I love him, and I'm sorry, Alex."

Handing her the keys, "Jess—don't run from something good. AJ loves you, and Alex, well, he will be ok in the end."

"Thanks, Mom. I just need some space. There is so much... stuff."

Glancing down at her belly, she couldn't believe her predicament. Her true love was back from the dead, yet she didn't feel they belonged together. And AJ... God, how she had fallen in love with him. All this pressure was too much. She had to get out of there. "And Jess?" She looked at her. "Get some sleep; you're carrying my grandbaby now."

"Wait... how?"

"A mother just knows these things. Don't worry—your secret is safe with me. You will tell them both when the time is right."

She kissed her forehead. "Drive safe. I'll tell them you weren't feeling well and drove home. A nice hot shower is just what you need."

"Thanks, Mom."

Turning, she pressed the elevator button. It seemed like an eternity waiting for the doors to open.

"Jess?" AJ stood behind her.

"AJ—I'm sorry. I just need some space. This is all too much right now."

"Fine, but let me take you home. You're in no condition to drive. Please?"

She debated for a minute. "Ok. Here, take these to your mom. But I'm serious, AJ—I need to be alone for a little while."

"I know."

He walked the keys to his mom, telling them he was taking her home. They got on the elevator together, AJ standing beside her, still giving her the space she had asked for. She could see the pain written on his face. She reached out and took his hand in hers, smiling as they walked off the elevator towards their car.

The ride home was somber. They didn't speak, though they never let go of each other's hand. As they pulled into the driveway, John walked over. "Jess, are you ok?"

"Yeah—I just need time." Hugging him, she turned and walked towards the house.

"Call me if you need anything—I love you, sis."

"Love you too. Thanks."

AJ and Jess walked into the room, and he closed the door behind them. Jesse couldn't even look at him. She was falling apart on the inside. "I'm going to take a bath. I just need to figure out some stuff."

"OK, I'll just grab a change of clothes and sleep in my old room."

Forcing a smile at him, she nodded. She could see how hard this was for him. He was trying to respect her and grant her wishes. "Thanks, AJ—I'm so sorry."

"Hey," he hugged her, "don't apologize. I told you I'd walk through fire for you, and this is nothing."

He kissed her head before letting go. They walked up the stairs together, and she watched him gather his things.

"If you need anything, call me. I will leave my door open. I love you, Jess."

He turned and walked out. Walking into the bathroom, she stripped off her clothes. Turning the water on, she looked herself over in the mirror. Pressing her hand to her belly, she smiled. "Little one, I promise to figure this out. You deserve that."

She slipped into the bath, soaking in the water until it became cool. Drying herself off, she slipped on one of AJ's t-shirts. His scent was strong, and she inhaled, relishing the memory of his arms. Pulling back the covers, she slipped into the bed. Glancing towards the door, she spotted the worn flag on her dresser. She couldn't help but laugh—it stood for nothing now.

Except maybe a giant mess up.

She lay there tossing and turning, unable to sleep. Her mind wandered to Alex, then AJ. She loved Alex, but it was different now. So much time had passed without him, and she'd moved on. AJ—he was the reason she had learned to live again. She loved him deeply, and here she was, separating herself from him. For what reason? Guilt? It wasn't fair to him. She cried herself to sleep. She did not know how or what she was supposed to do. Crush the man she loved now or break the man she once loved. Either way, someone was going to be hurt.

Chapter Twenty-One

THE MORNING LIGHT streamed through the window, waking Jess from her sleepless night. She stretched and slid from the bed, quickly going to the closet to pull on some clothes. Uncertain of what she was supposed to do, she knew she needed to face Alex back. She walked to her door, peering into AJ's room across the way. He was sprawled out on the bed, and the covers kicked off on the floor. God, he was beautiful.

Turning away, she walked down the stairs, debating how to get to the hospital. Before heading out, she left a note for AJ. Her heart ached in so many ways—fate seemed cruel to her twice over. Careful not to slam the door, she pulled it shut. She didn't see John approaching her, and turning, she bumped into him.

"Umph..."

John grabbed her to keep her from falling over. "Sorry—Jess, I was worried about you. I didn't mean to startle you."

"No, it's ok. I was just heading to your house. Can you take me to the base?"

"Isn't AJ taking you?"

Glancing down at her feet, "He's still sleeping—I... I didn't want to wake him. Plus, I need some time to think."

"Jess," John pulled her chin up to look into her eyes, "I know this is hard, but we are all here for you. And no matter what you decide, we will all support you."

"That's the thing. I don't know what I'm supposed to do."

The tears spilled freely from her already swollen eyes. He was pulling her into an embrace, "Jess. You don't have to decide anything today. Let's see, Alex. Talk with him. There's plenty of time to figure the rest out. Ok?"

"Yeah—sure. Let's go."

The ride to the base was ephemeral. Her thoughts were all over the place. Her nerves matched. "Good morning, Mrs. Holt. Alex has been asking for you."

Smiling, she nodded at the nurse. "Thanks."

Walking into his room, she found him standing by the window. He was thinner than she remembered him, but from the back, he was unmistakably her Alex. Turning to face her, "Jess."

They froze, staring at each other. Unable to move or speak, she just smiled. "God—You're beautiful."

Alex started towards her, limping slightly as he walked around the bed. Stopping before her, he brushed a loose strand of hair from her face. "I dreamed of this every day and night. The thought of being close to you again kept me sane." He leaned in. Before she could react, his lips pressed against hers. His tongue tickled her lips, slipping its way into her mouth.

Pushing away, "Alex, I...I can't. I'm sorry." She walked around him, sitting down on the edge of the bed.

He walked to sit beside her, taking her hand in his good hand. "I'm sorry, Jess. I... I just thought you'd want this."

"What is it, Jess? I thought everything could go back to normal. I'm home—here with you."

"Oh, Alex... Nothing is normal. It's been two years... Two. I buried you and mourned your death. I... I just need some time to figure this out, ok?" She searched his eyes, waiting to see his reaction.

"What are you saying? Wait—did you move on? Oh god... I'm so stupid. Of course, you did." He stood, throwing the pillow across the room.

"Alex, please... you have to understand this is difficult. I just need some time." He pushed past her, causing her to stumble, almost falling over.

"You need time? TIME? I was held hostage—hostage, Jess. Do you understand what that means? I held on to your face in my head... pushing to survive and get home to you, and you need time?" He grabbed her arm. "You're my wife—Jess. MY WIFE!"

Commander Wynn burst through the door, "Is everything alright in here?"

He looked at Alex, holding her arm, and her expression read, "Alex, son. You need to let her go and take a deep breath."

Alex glanced at his hand wrapped around her upper arm, releasing his grip. "Oh god, Jess... what have I done?"

She ran to Commander Wynn, allowing him to wrap her in a protective embrace. "Alex, I know this is hard for you, but you have to control your temper. You're scaring Jess—is that what you want?"

"No... I... I—what's wrong with me?" Alex sat down on the bed and dropped his head into his hands.

"You've been through a traumatic experience, son. This is to be expected, but you can't lash out at those who care about you. Things have changed, Alex. Nothing is like it was two years ago. You need to respect Jesse's wishes and give her time. She moved on, son—whether or not you want to hear that."

Alex looked up, searching Jess's face. "I'm sorry, Jess."

"Sorry for what?" AJ stepped into the room.

"AJ—I... I lost control."

"Jess," AJ pulled her from Commander Wynn's arms, "did he hurt you?" AJ looked over her body, inspecting her for injuries. His expression was fearful and angry, wrapped into one.

"No—he... he just got so angry."

Burying her head into his shoulder, she sobbed. AJ pulled her tighter. "Shhhhh... it's ok, Jess. I've got you. Alex didn't mean it—did you, Alex?"

"No—I'd never hurt you, Jess. I'm confused. Please... I couldn't live with myself if you were afraid of me."

Peeking out from AJ's hold, "I'm not afraid of you... Alex, I love you—I do, but everything has changed, and I need time to figure out what I should do. I moved on—and I'm in love. But I love you too. Do you understand?"

Alex's face morphed into rage. "Get out, *now!*"

AJ guided her to the hallway. Commander Wynn was moving toward the nurse's station. "Oh God, what have I done, AJ?"

"Nothing, Jess, you can't pretend everything is normal... It's not. Look—I get you. You need time to decide what you want. But I am not going anywhere, ok?" he lifted her chin to look into her eyes. "You have my heart—I will support your decision no matter what. Even if it kills me." He smiled, wiping away some of the tears taking residence on her cheeks.

"AJ." She rested her forehead against his. "I love you... I'm so confused."

Chapter Twenty-Two

THE NEXT FEW weeks became a blur for Jess. Alex was back, not as a memory, but physically at the base hospital. School had ended for the summer, and everyone awaited the arrival of John and Allie's boys.

"Jess," AJ entered the kitchen, "John just called me. Allie's water broke."

"What? Let's go—take me to the hospital." Jess stood, realizing she wasn't even dressed. "Well, let me go get some clothes on. I'll be right back."

Walking by AJ, he grabbed her. "I like you dressed in my shirt."

Kissing her, he released her. "AJ—I promise I will figure my shit out soon. Alex is due to be released from the hospital this week, and maybe, just maybe, I can work through these messed up emotions."

Hurrying up the stairs, Jess closed the door behind her. She had been wearing loose clothes for the last several weeks, trying to hide her baby bump that had popped out. She still hadn't told anyone except Alex's mom. She was the one who went with her when she went to her first official appointment. She was five months along, and how she had kept it hidden this long was a miracle. It had been almost nine weeks since Alex had returned from the dead. AJ had moved back into his old room, respecting her desire for space. Her mind was constantly confused. Grabbing a pair of leggings, she slipped on a t-shirt dress. Looking in the mirror, she knew she would need to make some decisions soon. This baby was about to blow her secret wide open.

"Jess, you ready?" AJ called out from the other side of the door.

"Yeah." She pulled the door open. "Let's go meet our nephews!"

The fifteen-minute ride to the local hospital felt normal for the first time. AJ reached for her hand, wrapping his fingers around hers. Smiling, she glanced up at him to see him watching her.

"What?"

"You're beautiful, you know that? There's something different about you, Jess."

Swallowing, "Different? What do you mean?"

"I don't know... just different. I know you needed your space, but it's been nearly two months—I want to take you out. Can I do that?"

"AJ..." She shook her head and said, "Let's meet our nephews first—then we can talk. Ok?"

They walked into the hospital holding hands, so wrapped up in the moment that they didn't notice Alex standing with his parents. "Jess."

She snatched her hand from AJ's, blushing as she approached him.

"Alex," she hugged him quickly, "I didn't know you were getting out today."

"Yeah—the doctor said I was good to go. And since John is welcoming his first baby... babies, I wanted to come. Dad picked me up an hour ago." Alex turned to AJ. "Thanks for bringing my wife to the hospital."

The two stood there, staring at each other like a Mexican standoff. The silence was deafening. "Umm... Alex, we talked about this. I'm not your wife—not really. And AJ lives with me, so it made sense for us to come together."

"Right–I forgot you've been living with Jess playing house. Well... I'm back, so you won't need to do that anymore."

"Can we discuss this later? I am here to see my nephews and their parents."

She pushed past the two men, acting like children. Both had a piece of her glass heart. It was fragile and in danger of cracking again. Both men were important to her, but deciding which one she was meant to be with was going to kill her. The only thing holding her together right now was the baby she carried. Pressing the elevator button, she felt someone standing behind her.

Never turning around, "What—I can't deal with any more crap."

"I'm sorry, Jess. My temper is still something I work on. I know AJ has helped you with my absence."

"Where is AJ?"

"He and my parents went for a walk. I asked them to give me a few minutes with you." They boarded the elevator together. Pressing the button for the maternity floor, Jess felt a sense of longing—she had a baby of her own to think about.

"Alex," looking at him, "I don't know where we stand anymore. I love you—I never stopped. But I moved on... I gave my heart to someone else. And just because you are back, I can't turn off those feelings. I am in love with someone else. Do you understand?"

He didn't respond. Instead, he pressed the stop button and pulled her flush against his body. "Then I need to make you remember why you want me." His lips crashed into hers, his tongue darting between her lips. The walls she had erected crumpled as she melted into his hold. His hands roamed her backside, running up her arms as he pulled her tighter against him.

"Alex..." she pushed off him. "I can't...I'm sorry." Tears threatened to spill as she caught her breath.

"Why Jess—tell me one reason I can't have a chance to win your heart all over."

She knew there was only one thing she could say. The elevator doors opened, and she glanced back at him as she stepped out. "Because Alex, I'm pregnant."

He stepped off, grabbing her arm. "What? What do you mean, you're pregnant?"

"Exactly what it means, Alex. I'm having someone else's baby."

John ran out to greet her. "Jess!" pulling her into a hug, she peeked at Alex from under John's arms. He was stunned, standing still, staring at her.

"Well?? Is Allie ok? The babies?"

"Yeah, she's good. They had to do a C-section, but everything turned out great—well, except…"

"Except what? John, is something wrong with the babies?"

"No—nothing like that. It's just I don't have two sons."

Jesse blinked in confusion. "Wait, you didn't have twins?"

John's smile beamed—he lit up the room. "Yeah, I had twins. Those dumbasses had the sex wrong, though. I have a son and a daughter."

"Seriously? WOW, that's great!" She pulled him into a hug again. "Well, what did you name them?"

"Hunter after dad, and Harper. Allie named her. She's so beautiful, Jess. You can come back in a little while. They are cleaning the babies up and getting Allie settled in her room. I'm going to head back—tell everyone for me, ok?"

"Sure! Kiss Allie for me, ok?"

Scanning the room again, she found Alex watching her. He started towards her when the elevator doors opened.

"Well? Do we have any babies?" Don and Betty hurried toward her, AJ walking behind them.

"Yes—but." She smiled. "He has a daughter and a son! They were wrong about the sexes."

"A girl and a boy! That's fantastic." Don clapped his hands together.

AJ grabbed her hand and smiled as he moved into the waiting room.

"I can't wait to hold my grandbaby." Betty smiled as she stared at her.

"Well," Alex pushed off the wall, "You might get your wish, Mom."

"Alex." She gritted her teeth, shooting him a look of warning.

"What do you mean, Alex?" Don asked.

"It would appear my wife... oh, I'm sorry, she's not my wife anymore... regardless, she's pregnant. Isn't that right, Jess?"

Don turned to look at her. "Is he serious?"

"I... I..." words failed her. Her eyes pleaded with Alex to stop.

"Yep—my dear old wife is knocked up. Care to tell us who the dad is, Jess?"

AJ stood off to the side, face ashen, staring at her wide-eyed. "Alex. Please don't do this here."

AJ broke the silence. "Is he telling the truth? Are you pregnant?" He moved closer to her, his eyes fixated on her belly. Surely, they could all see the swell of life she was hiding.

"I was going to tell you... I just didn't know how... I mean—I didn't plan this."

"Why would AJ need to know?" Alex glared at his brother before the realization dawned on him. "Oh... I see," Alex walked forward, "You've been playing house for real, little brother. Even down to fucking my wife."

AJ moved in a flash, his fist connecting with Alex's jaw. "Don't talk about her like that... She mourned you, Alex—she almost died from grief. We didn't plan for your death. And." He moved to stand in front of her. "We didn't plan to fall in love like this—it just happened." He took her hand in his. "She didn't ask to be a widow. She didn't ask to deal with your death."

"Well, I'm not dead—am I?"

"Boys," Don moved between them, "This isn't the time or place to have this discussion. Alex, come with me. I'll take you home."

"Home... that's funny, dad. My home was with her. Now—I don't have a home." Alex turned and stormed towards the elevators.

"Alex, please," she rushed towards him, grabbing his arm. "I love you. I do, but AJ saved me, and I love him—he has my heart now... I'm so sorry."

"Let. Go. Of. Me." Alex snatched his arm from her hold. "Fuck you, Jess. I held onto our love. It saved me. But you're dead to me now."

Storming into the open elevator, Don walked towards him, placing his hand on her shoulder, "It will be ok, Jess."

She watched the doors close, her heart cracking as it did. She loved AJ, but her heart broke for Alex at that moment.

"Jess," AJ stood behind her as she stared at the closed elevator. "Please." He placed his hands on her shoulders. "Talk to me."

Slowly, she turned to face him, unsure of what she was supposed to say. She had been lying to him—hell, she'd been lying to herself. Hiding the truth, he deserved to know. Her hand gently covered the tiny swell starting to protrude. "I... I'm sorry I lied to you."

The sob escaping her lips was for the man whose heart she ripped in two and the other for the baby she now carried. "Don't." AJ pulled her to him. "Don't you dare apologize, Jess. This—this is just more than any one person should deal with. I should have noticed. I... I just thought you were depressed. I didn't once think you were carrying my baby." He stepped back from their embrace and pressed his hand to her belly. He let out a slight gasp as tears gathered in his eyes.

"I shouldn't have lied... you deserved to know. I just didn't know how to tell you or Alex. I crushed him."

"We're having a baby." It was more of a statement than a question. He stared at her in wonder, searching her eyes for something. She knew immediately he was looking for love—wondering if she still loved him or if the baby was all that bound them together.

"Yes. We are having a baby." She leaned into his hand and pressed her lips to his. "It's you, AJ. You're what I want—who I want. I love Alex, yes. But not like I love you. Maybe I did a long time ago, but things change... people change. I just didn't want to hurt him. He's been through enough hurt already."

"Jess..." He broke into a sob, pulling her close to his body while he cried against her. They stood at the elevators, holding each other as they shed tears. Tears of sadness, tears of happiness, but most of all, tears of love.

Their love radiated in that moment—like a beacon of light cutting through the dark. They pulled each other through the worst possible experience in life, only to find a deep-seated love. And now—a life grew inside her as a symbol of that love.

"Um, Jess?" John had come out looking for her. He stood by the nurse's station, waiting for her to respond.

"John, everything ok?" She pulled away from AJ, straightening her shirt and wiping her tear-stained face off her sleeve.

"Seriously? You're bawling in the middle of the hospital, and you ask if everything's alright?"

"Guess that seems silly. AJ." She pulled AJ's hand, tugging him to stand against her again. "And I have something to tell you. I didn't want to do this now—but you heard the commotion."

"Well, yeah. I know something happened with Alex. Betty told me to find you and ask myself. Did he do something to hurt you? Before I forget, you can come back to see Allie and your niece and nephew now."

"Then let's go back there... I'd rather just tell you both at the same time. Come on, AJ, let's meet our niece and nephew." She emphasized 'our'—wanting to reassure him he was it for her. Alex would always be a part of her life, but life was different now.

"Wait—does this mean you've decided what to do? I mean, with AJ and Alex?" John stared at her as she walked ahead of him.

"Yep—I already knew... I just needed to figure out how to tell everyone without hurting Alex. But I screwed that part up."

They walked into Allie's room. She was holding Harper in her arms. Hunter was sleeping in the tiny bassinet next to her bed.

"Jess—you can't just say that and walk off. What do you mean, you screwed up?" John followed her into the room.

"Hush. Let me see the babies. We can talk in a minute."

She walked over to Allie. "She's beautiful. You look amazing, Allie."

"Thanks—you want to hold your niece?"

"Yes, please." She took the tiny bundle from her arms, unable to take her eyes off her perfect face. She was small, wrapped in a pink blanket, and her beautiful dark hair peeked out of the baby cap she wore. She couldn't contain the emotions. Tears spilled from her eyes as she marveled at the tiny human in her arms.

"You look like a natural." John beamed at her as she cradled his daughter against her chest.

As she rocked Harper against her, Hunter stirred in his bassinet. John scooped him up and thrust him into AJ's arms. "Here—might as well get comfortable holding one of these..."

She looked at him, catching the slight wink he gave her. "You know?"

"Jess—you're my sister. It's been my job to watch out for you since mom and dad died. Plus, you may think you're hiding it in your baggy shirts, but that tiny life inside you wants to be seen. So... yeah—I know. How far along are you, sis?"

"Wait... How did I not notice? I feel like a bigger ass now." AJ shook his head.

"AJ, you were so worried about her mental state that you brushed off the baggy clothes as depression. But I just suspected—and when I heard Alex blow up... I knew I was right."

"Five months," her response was barely audible as she spoke.

"What did you say?" AJ looked up from Hunter, who was sound asleep, cradled in his arms.

"I'm five months. When Alex was brought home, I got sick while we were at the base—well, I wasn't. Not really, anyway. I was eight weeks pregnant. I didn't know what to do, so I hid it from everyone. Except for Betty. She went with me to the doctor."

"Are you telling me that my mom knew and didn't tell me?"

AJ had placed Hunter back into his bassinet and walked to stand in front of her. She handed Harper back to John and smiled. "Yeah—she knew it wasn't her secret to tell. And I am glad she found out... I needed her."

She walked to the chair in the corner where Betty had placed her bag. Digging into her wallet, she pulled a tiny black-and-white picture out. Thrusting her hand into AJ, "Here's a picture of our baby."

AJ took the picture from her grasp, holding it like glass. His eyes were glistening with tears as he took in the tiny image. "Do you know what we are having?"

"No... that appointment is this week. I planned on telling you tonight. I just..." Turning away from him, she faced the window, hiding her sorrowful expression from everyone.

"What—Jess, baby... please don't hide from us."

"Jess, you're having a baby." Allie's voice was happy, "We will have kids close in age together... They will grow up together!"

She was right. She was being silly, but she felt so guilty about how she'd hurt Alex. "That's true. And I am happy. But I didn't want to hurt anyone. By lying, I hurt everyone."

AJ grabbed her, spinning her to look into his eyes. "You listen to me... You did what you had to do in this unbelievably hard situation. Stop blaming yourself and realize that we all love you—I. Love. You."

"He's right, you know. And if I'm being honest... I am glad you are with AJ. Alex isn't the same man he was, Jess. I don't think he will ever be."

"She's right." Don walked into the room, followed by Betty.

"Don, oh god. How is he?"

"Hurt, mad. Hell, he's angrier than hurt, I think. Angry at the world for robbing him of his life. Angry at you, angry at AJ— but mostly angry at himself."

"Angry at himself? Why on earth would he be angry at himself? I'm the one that hurt him. Not the other way around."

"See, that's where you're wrong, Jess," Don walked towards AJ. "He's angry for expecting life to be the way it was. He's angry for not realizing you did exactly as he asked you to do... move on and love again. He's angry at AJ for being the one to hold your heart. But in time—he'll get over all those emotions. We just have to give him time. Now... Let me see my grandbabies."

Don walked over to Allie and took Harper from her arms. He considered Allie and John's family as well, so naturally, he thought of Harper and Hunter as his grandbabies. Betty was busy fussing over Hunter. Watching them with the babies made her heart happy. They would be great-grandparents.

Her eyes searched the room, coming to rest on AJ, who was watching her. "What?"

"You. Are. Beautiful."

She blushed, "No, I'm not. John, Allie," she looked to her brother, standing by his wife, "I'm going to leave you two. Kiss those babies for me. I'll call you tomorrow. Ok?"

"Alright, sis. I love you! And remember, we support you in every way possible. Let us know if you need anything."

Nodding, she slipped out of the room, AJ following closely behind her. "You want me to take you home?"

"No, AJ."

He stopped, stunned at her answer. "Oh... Ok."

"AJ." She laced her fingers in his. "I want you to come home with me. I'm sorry I pushed you away."

"Home? You mean like with you, with you?"

"Yes—like I want you back in *our* bed."

AJ pressed the elevator button. "Damn, this thing takes forever!"

"Calm down—we have the rest of our lives, AJ."

"Jess, I've spent the last eight weeks away from you... but now, I just want to get you home."

He pressed himself against her, catching her mouth with his. His tongue was needy against hers. She could feel his erection pressing against her thigh, eliciting a moan to escape between her parted lips. The elevator doors opened, and AJ pulled her in with him. "God, I love you, woman."

"I love you too, AJ."

They stood, hands entwined, as the elevator descended. It seemed to take an eternity for the doors to open and let them free.

Even though her heart broke for Alex and the pain she had caused him, the love she felt from AJ kept the fragile glass piece it had become from shattering completely.

Chapter Twenty-Three

THE FIFTEEN-MINUTE RIDE home felt more like fifty minutes. AJ never let go of Jess's hand except to get in the car. As they pulled into the driveway, she felt a sense of foreboding. Something just seemed off.

"AJ—something's wrong. I know I left lights on when we left."

"Yeah... I know. Stay in the car while I go check it out." He kissed her as he got out of the car. She slipped from the passenger side and stood, leaning against the door.

"Please be careful—maybe I should just call John."

"I'll be fine. It's nothing."

As AJ slipped into the house, Jess quickly called John, asking him to send someone over anyway. Waiting for AJ was nearly impossible. When he finally emerged from the house, his expression was sorrowful.

"Jess, did you call John?"

"AJ, what is it? What's wrong?"

"Jess—I think Alex was here. The house is empty now... but..."

"But what? What makes you think that?"

"There are some things that have been destroyed."

She walked around him, making her way up the stairs. "What do you mean, destroyed?"

"Jess, please don't go inside—let me wait for whoever John is sending. Ok?" AJ moved to stand between her and the open doorway.

"No, AJ. What is it?" She pushed past him.

Her breath hitched as she stepped into the foyer. The walls had been spray-painted with 'whore', and several pictures she had hung were lying on the ground shattered. She made her way up the stairs. As she went inside her room, AJ grabbed her arm.

"Please, Jess—Don't go in there."

She snatched her arm free, pushing open her door. "AJ, what did he do?"

There on the bed were the charred remains of the flag she had been given at Alex's funeral. In the center of the pile of ashes were his dog tags. He had shredded the bed linens and burned them, along with the one piece of memorabilia she had of his death. Above the bed, he had scrawled *whore.*

She crumpled to the floor, sobs ripping through her body. "Why... why would he do this?"

AJ kneeled beside her. "He's lost, Jess. He needs someone to blame. I'm so sorry, baby." He held her as she cried into his chest.

"Hello?" A male voice called from downstairs.

"We're upstairs."

A uniformed deputy came in, eyes wide as he entered the bedroom scene. "Is everyone ok? Ma'am? Sheriff Ryan called and asked if we would come over. Something about a possible break-in... was this how you found the house?"

"Yes, Deputy. I am sure my brother did this. That was his flag. He's having a hard time coming back to life, and anger controls him right now."

She continued to sob in AJ's arms, "This is my fault."

"This is not your fault, Jess. Don't say that. Alex is angry right now, and what he has done is messed up."

AJ stood, pulling her off the floor. He walked them across the hall to his room, which was completely untouched. He pushed through the partially open door, guiding her to the bed. "Lay down. I'll take care of this mess. You need to rest. This stress can't be good for you or our baby."

He was right. She let him lay her on the bed and pull the covers up. Placing a kiss on her head, "I'll be right downstairs talking to the deputy. Get some rest, baby. You can't do anything right now."

AJ pulled the door closed, leaving her in the dark. His curtains left little light streaming in, making the room almost black. Her eyes grew heavy as she dozed off, thinking about Alex and how she hurt him. Her sleep was fitful as she tossed and turned under the covers. The bed smelled of AJ, giving her some comfort, but the other part needed to see what had been ruined. Slipping out from under the covers, she padded towards the door. She stopped at the closed door and heard talking just beyond it.

"Why would he do this, Dad?"

"Son, he's hurting. He lost two years of his life, and now—he's lost Jess. It's a lot to take. He will eventually get over his anger, and when he does, he will regret doing this to the both of you. But for now, you are going to have to leave him alone. He has agreed to move on base. Commander Wynn convinced him. It's for the best. He needs to find his place in the world again —without the woman he loved... loves."

"Dad... I love him, too. I didn't mean to hurt him."

"Deep down, I believe he knows that—just give him time, ok?"

AJ sighed, "Yeah—what do I tell Jess? The things he did... she saw all that."

She emerged from the room. "You don't have to tell me anything."

"Jess, how much did you hear?"

"Everything. And AJ. I don't blame him for this," she waved her hands in the air, "He's hurting, and I am sorry for that."

Don spoke, his eyes weary with concern. "Jess—you're an amazing woman. Don't you dare think for a second you did anything to deserve this? You and AJ have every right to love each other, and you should." Don stepped forward, pressing his palm to the swell of her stomach. "So—this is my grandbaby?"

"Yes. Looks like you're going to be a grandpa."

"Awe, hell—John is just as much my son as you are my daughter. It's just nice to have a blood grandbaby. But despite the blood, Harper and Hunter are my grandbabies, too." He smiled, pulling his hand from her belly. "Jess, we love you. And no matter what happens to Alex, you and AJ belong together—with or without this baby. You understand?"

"Yeah," she smiled at AJ, "I do. Thanks, Dad."

He kissed her and hugged AJ. "Let me know what I can do to help. Take care of her, son."

"I will, Dad. I will."

Don left, leaving AJ and her standing in the hallway. He smiled at her and pressed his hand to her belly. "You hungry?"

"Starving."

"Come on. I'm going to fix you some dinner."

She sat at the table while he fixed stir-fry, salivating at the delicious smell. She took her last bite and said, "That was delicious, thanks."

"Are you ready for some dessert?"

"No way, I'm stuffed."

"Guess it's a good thing. I don't mean food." AJ scooped her off the chair and carried her up the stairs. She rested her head on his shoulder, enjoying the closeness of being in his arms.

"I think I've changed my mind," she smiled at him. "I may want two servings of dessert."

AJ kicked the door open and then slammed it shut with his foot. He laid her down on his bed.

"Good thing I have enough." AJ loomed over her. "God, you're beautiful." Grasping his neck, she pulled his mouth to hers. Their lips collided, tongues exploring each other. Her fingers entwined in his hair, and a soft moan escaped with their kisses.

"I love you, AJ."

Slowly, he undressed her, slipping her panties down her legs. His lips brushed the slight swell of her belly before dipping between her legs. The warmth of his breath sent shivers through her core. With a little flick of his tongue, he slipped between her pink folds.

She arched against him, pressing her hips against his shoulders. Writhing under his mouth, she couldn't stop the sounds of pleasure. "AJ, I need you."

He smiled against her flesh. "You sure?"

"Yes—please!"

Climbing up her body, she hadn't noticed he'd stripped off his pants as well. Kissing her, he propped himself up on his elbows and paused. "What? AJ, is there something wrong?"

"I don't want to hurt you."

Running her hand down his face, "Baby, you can't hurt me or the baby. Now, make love to me."

Pressing his lips to hers once more, he eased himself into her, filling her up to the hilt. She moved against him, grinding her clit against his pelvic bone. His movements sped up, and before she knew it, she was climaxing again. AJ continued pressing into the innermost part of her. His kisses were urgent and full of need. Thrusting against him, she could feel herself squeezing against his hardened cock.

"AJ—I can't hold on much longer."

"Come with me, baby."

He grunted, pressing into her one last time as her walls tightened around him, forcing his seed into her core. She screamed out as they came together. Collapsing on the bed beside her, AJ pressed his hand to her belly. He gently tickled her bump as he pulled her against his side.

"When can we find out what the baby is?"

"Actually... I have an appointment tomorrow. I was going to tell you tonight, but Alex ruined it. Will you come to the appointment with me?"

"He didn't ruin anything, Jess—and of course I'll go. I wouldn't miss it for the world."

She snuggled into him, relishing the warmth of his body. He fingered her hair, causing her to relax, and her eyes droop. It didn't take long before sleep claimed her again. It seemed like she only slept for an hour, but by the color of the walls in their room, it was obvious the sun was rising. AJ had his arm draped over her as he slept. She smiled, knowing he would be with her for life.

"AJ." She pressed her lips to his forehead. "Baby, we need to get up and get dressed. I need to get to the appointment in a little while."

She glanced at the clock, noting it was six-thirty. Her appointment was at eight. Lucky for them, the office was only a ten-minute drive. "AJ—seriously, we need to get dressed." She slung his arm off her and slipped from the bed. Heading towards the shower, she turned to see him staring at her. "What? Why are you staring at me? It's creepy?"

"Creepy?" he threw his pillow at her. "I love watching you."

"Fine... whatever, we need to hurry."

Closing the bathroom door, she took a quick shower. She pulled her hair into a ponytail and wrapped a towel around herself. "Your turn!"

AJ grabbed her and kissed her hard, slipping his tongue into her mouth. His erection pressed against her belly. "Whoa, now... we don't have time for that. Don't you want to see what the baby will be?"

"You're right. But damn—you're so irresistible!"

Chuckling, he headed into the shower. She slipped on a loose-fitting dress and sandals. As she was buckling her strap, AJ emerged from the bathroom. His towel wrapped around his waist, showing off his clearly defined muscles. "You look yummy... I wish we didn't have to rush out."

AJ tossed the towel at her. "Feast your eyes out, woman."

She watched as he dressed. He was a sight to see—and he was all hers. Once he was done, he took her by the hand, leading her out of the bedroom.

"Let's go—I can't wait to see our baby!"

Chapter Twenty-Four

THEY SAT ANXIOUSLY in the waiting room, awaiting the nurse to call them back. Jess's nerves were taut, and she didn't care about the baby's gender; she just longed for a healthy child.

"Mrs. Holt." Rising, she took AJ's hand and followed the nurse to the back. "Alright," the nurse patted the examination table. "Hop up here and roll your dress up so we can see your belly better." Jess complied, and the nurse draped sheets across her chest and legs. "That should keep you warm. The doctor should be here in just a few minutes."

"Thank you." Jess smiled at her as the door closed.

AJ moved to stand beside her, curling his fingers into hers. "I don't care what the baby is—boy or girl, I'll be happy," he said, pressing his lips to her knuckles.

The OB, Dr. Finn, walked in, eyeing AJ curiously. Jess introduced AJ as the baby's father and her fiancé.

"Good to meet you. I am glad she settled. The stress of her personal life was not good for the baby."

AJ shook his hand. "Yes, sir. I am, too—for more than one reason."

"Alright, ready to see what you're having, and when may this little one be making his or her appearance?"

"YES!" AJ and Jess said in unison.

"Jess, this is going to feel a little cool." The doctor applied cold jelly on Jess's swollen abdomen. The ultrasound revealed a surprising revelation. "Well... Humm."

"What? Is there something wrong?" AJ stood taller, stiffening.

"No... not wrong—just surprising. I am not sure how we missed this with the first ultrasound."

"What do you mean?" Jess asked, trying to see the screen.

"Well, Jesse. You're not having a baby."

"What? What do you mean I'm not having a baby? Look at me... is it cancer? A tumor?"

Chuckling, the doctor clarified, "No, sorry. I mean, there's not just one baby. Jess, you're having twins." He turned the screen towards them, revealing two perfectly shaped babies.

"Twins," AJ said matter of fact. "Two babies?"

Jess squeezed his hand. "AJ—we're having two." Her smile illuminated the room.

"Yep. Two. And from the looks of things, they're identical. It would appear they share the same amniotic sac and placenta. Let me check some measurements, and then we can talk about the remaining months of your pregnancy."

AJ leaned down and kissed Jess's forehead. "Marry me."

"AJ—I already said yes."

"No—Marry me today at the courthouse. I don't want a big wedding. I only want you and our babies. Please... I don't want them born to unwed parents." Overwhelmed with love, Jess agreed.

He kissed her passionately. "Ahem," the doctor cleared his throat, "Alright, everything looks good. Your sons will be here around October 10th."

The doctor handed AJ some photos. "Here are some pictures of them."

"Wait—you said, sons?"

"Yep. They weren't shy. They let those third legs hang out wide open. See here?" He pointed to something on the print-out. "That's not a leg or the umbilical cord. That, my dear man, is his penis. And Jess, I'd say you're closer to six months from their size."

AJ grinned. "You're giving me two sons."

Jess pulled her dress down over her stomach. "Six months? How is that possible? I am not nearly large enough for six months."

"Twin B is seated far back—have you had back pain?"

"Yeah—a little." Jess shrugged her shoulders.

"Well, that's how. But I venture to say that in the next week, that will change. He's going to start to feel cramped and move around and make that slight bump, not so slight. You make sure you take it easy. I'll see you back in 2 weeks. Also, I am not sure you should return to work, but we can talk in August when you are close to returning.”

“Ok. Thanks, Dr. Finn.”

AJ helped Jess stand, pulling her into a hug. “Thank you, baby. Let’s go get married.”

They walked out of the office together, both floating on the high of the pending arrivals of their babies.

THEY GOT MARRIED at the courthouse, just as they had planned. AJ’s parents and John and Allie were upset about it. However, they reassured everyone that they would have a proper wedding after the babies arrived.

Allie, as a mother, was adorable. The twins kept both John and Allie busy, and Jesse found it amusing while secretly taking notes for her and AJ’s twins’ impending arrival.

September arrived quickly, and Jesse’s belly had tripled in size. The decision was made for her to take a year off from work. Although sad about not returning to teaching, the growing belly reminded her of more important priorities.

Alex was living with his parents and rarely seen. His struggles with depression and PTSD led him to avoid the narrator and AJ. It was for the best, given the tense dynamics.

AJ resumed work, commuting between home and the base daily. The old room was converted into a nursery, and the narrator was attempting last-minute decorations. Despite AJ’s request to leave it for him, she insisted on doing it herself.

“Jess, please leave that stuff for me. I will do it when I get home,” AJ begged her through the phone.

"AJ—I'm pregnant, not crippled. I want to do this... I promise I will be careful."

AJ sighed through the line, "Fine—but watch it, and don't stand on the ladder. Leave it for me if you can't hang it standing there. Deal?"

Silently shaking her head, "Yeah, yeah... I love you, AJ. Call me later, ok? I want to get this done and then take a nap."

"Alright. I love you."

After the phone conversation with AJ, Jesse hung pictures on the nursery wall. She attempted to reach for the last picture over the crib but fell when the chair shifted. Landing on her side, she felt a searing pain in her stomach and discovered blood was wetting the carpet.

She stretched as far as the pain allowed and fingered her phone, which had fallen on the floor. Grasping at the device, she swiped the screen and hit the first number that popped up. As she lay there in pain, she muttered into the phone before darkness consumed her.

Unaware of how long she lay there, Jesse woke to the sensation of being shaken. "Jess—god damn it... open your eyes." Faintly, she could hear the shuffling of feet. "Yeah, she's on the floor. Tell them the door is open. There's a lot of blood. No. No. Look, she's pregnant—due in... AH Fuck, I don't know."

Whoever was there was familiar, but she couldn't open her eyes—she was too weak to do anything.

"I'm not the daddy. NO! God Damn it, what does that matter? Are the paramedics close? Jess, baby, can you hear me?"

Jesse blinked, the room coming into a blurry focus. She tried to sit up. "Did you hit your head? Jess…"

Her hand went to my belly, wincing in pain as she recalled falling off the chair.

"No."

"Jess, AJ is on his way. The paramedics, too."

"AJ?" Shaking the fog from her brain, her eyes cleared, taking in the person kneeling beside me.

"Alex?"

"Jess, please lay still—you're losing a lot of blood."

She grabbed Alex's shirt as a tearing pain scorched its way through her belly. "FUCK"

"I think she is in labor… Tell them to hurry."

"OH MY GOD… The babies…" Jesse began crying.

"Look, Jess, I need to check you, ok? The 911 operator needs me to see if the babies are crowning. Can I check?"

"Alex, I'm scared."

He helped Jesse lay back down, pressing his phone against his shoulder, "What do I do?"

He pulled her skirt up and pushed her knees apart. "I think I see a head. You want me to do what?"

Another pain hit Jesse, and she felt like she needed to push. Alex's eyes widened, and he screamed, "Jess—NO! Stop pushing! She needs to push."

Alex looked terrified. Jesse grunted between the contractions. "Alex… why are you here?"

"Jess—the operator says you need to push when you can, ok?"

"No. I don't want to have this baby here... not without AJ. Alex, why are you HERE—" Another pain hit her.

"Those are contractions, Jess. I'm here because you called Dad's house but didn't say anything. After a while, I got worried and came over. I'm glad I did. Now push, ok?" Nodding, unable to argue anymore, she pushed. "That's it—one more, and I think he will be out."

Another contraction hit, and Jesse pushed with all her might, screaming as she did. "Here he comes, oh God... Jess." The cries of a tiny baby broke the grunts and screams. Jesse glanced down. Seeing Alex with their baby cradled in his arms brought a calmness over her body.

"Ok... I can tear my shirt." She heard him tell the person on the phone. Alex tore his shirt, tying off the umbilical cord. He grabbed a baby blanket that hung on the crib nearby, wrapping the tiny infant up. As another pain hit them, people rushing up the stairs invaded their ears.

"In here!" Alex called out as the paramedics stormed into the room.

Jesse let out a scream as a ripping pain tore through their body. "Please... something's wrong."

The paramedic took the baby from Alex. His partner kneeled at their feet. "We need to get her to the ambulance fast. Can you help me with her? I'm worried her placenta is rupturing."

Alex stood, bending to his knees. He scooped her off the floor. "Lead the way. I have her."

She rested their head against him. "I'm sorry, Alex."

"Hush now... no more apologies. Let's get you to the hospital."

Taking the steps two at a time, Alex hopped into the ambulance. The paramedic hopped in, holding the tiny infant, and closed the doors behind himself. "Look, we need to transport her and can't wait for another bus. You'll have to hold the baby while I tend to her, ok?"

Alex took their tiny son in his arms. "Ok... Jess, he's beautiful. He looks like AJ."

Jesse smiled, the dizziness consuming her. "Tell AJ I love him," as she started to fade, the sound of Alex's pained voice filled the inside of the ambulance.

"Jess—you'll tell him. My brother needs you... your sons need you. So, you fight and stay awake, ok? Don't you close your eyes."

The darkness took her. Jesse couldn't resist the temptation of the serenity it brought with it. The pain was too much to bear, so she gave in and closed her eyes.

Chapter Twenty-Five

SHE DRIFTED into a realm of peacefulness. It was calm but lonely. The beckoning from the distance fought the weight in her eyes. Slowly opening them and blinking into focus, she took in the sight before her. Alex was propped against the wall, still covered in blood. AJ sat next to her bed, holding her hand. The steady beep of machines startled her as she realized where she was.

"My babies... are they ok?"

"Jess!" AJ stood, kissed her head, and pulled her into a hug. His tears spilled down his face, dripping onto her cheek.

"AJ—why are you crying? Did something happen to the boys?"

"No... no, they're fine, Jess. It's you... we almost lost you—I almost lost you. We might have lost you all if it hadn't been for Alex." AJ stepped aside, giving her a clear view of Alex, who looked like he hadn't showered in a day. He smiled at her from his spot against the wall.

"Thank you."

"Jess, I am so sorry for the way I treated you. You and AJ deserve the happiness you have. Can you forgive me?"

Alex made his way slowly towards her bed. "Alex, you don't have to apologize. If anything—I should. I should have told you from the beginning, but I didn't want to hurt you—but I did, anyway."

"Jess—can we be friends?"

"Alex... we were always friends, but we're more than that. We're family."

He leaned down and kissed her forehead, turning to AJ. "Can you forgive me, brother?"

AJ pulled him into a hug. "You saved her, Alex. And there is nothing to forgive. We're brothers."

The nurse came in. "I need to check her vitals."

Alex headed towards the door. "I'll let everyone know she's awake and give you a while with her. They'll want to see you two soon, though."

"Thanks, Alex."

"Now—would you like to meet our sons? They need names, after all."

The nurse checked her vitals and sutures. She had an emergency C-section to deliver Twin B, who had been stuck behind the placenta that tore when she fell. Neither baby was injured, thank God. After checking her over, the nurse wheeled in two tiny bassinets. Even though she had delivered the babies four weeks early, they were a good size. Twin A was four pounds, five ounces, and Twin B was five pounds. His size made it more difficult to deliver vaginally, especially with the placenta issue.

AJ smiled at the babies cradled in her arms. "Well, what do you want to name them?"

"Well, I think Colton works. You liked that name, so how about Colton John?"

"Yeah, I like it. What about this guy?" AJ took Twin B from her arms.

"I'd like to name him after the man who helped him come into this world. What do you think?" She watched AJ for his reaction.

He looked at her with wide eyes. "Are you sure?"

"Yes. I'd like to name him Alexander Mika Holt."

"I like it. Alex. What do you think, little guy?" AJ stared down at his son, his grin radiating through the room. "And you, little fella... you like your name?"

AJ sat on the edge of the bed, cradling Alex in his arms. The happiness she felt was more than she deserved. She never thought she'd be here in her life. The last two years were a whirlwind of trials, but looking at her husband and boys, she knew she was finally at peace. A knock at the door gave way to their family. They all piled into the room, smiling at the two lives they brought into the world.

"Jess, how are you?" Allie hugged her as John shook AJ's hand.

"Tired, sore, but happy."

Everyone took turns passing the boys around. Even Alex had come back into the room. "Well, what are my grandson's names?" Don quirked an eyebrow at AJ.

"Jess—you want to do the honors?"

"Betty, that little bundle you're holding is Colton John." She smiled at her brother, his face reddening and eyes welling up with tears.

"Seriously, sis? Thank you," shaking AJ's hand.

"And Alex," everyone turned to Alex, who was cradling the baby he brought into the world, "That baby, the one you delivered, is Alexander Mika."

It took a moment to sink in. "Wait, Alex?"

"Yep—we decided he should be named after the man that helped him into the world. A man who I loved, no love, and someone who will be a big part of his life. Is that ok?"

Alex's tears rolled down his cheeks. "I can't tell you how honored I am. Thank you. Jess, AJ, I promise to protect this little guy and be the best uncle ever." He squeezed Alex to his chest, kissing his head before handing him over to AJ. "I am going to head out. Leave you two alone. Thank you again. I don't deserve it."

Not long after Alex left, everyone else followed suit, leaving her and AJ alone with their sons. "I love you, AJ."

"I love you, Jess. I don't know what I would do if I had lost you."

He leaned in and kissed her lips. "I'm sorry I worried you. I'm not going anywhere, though—you're stuck with me forever."

"I wouldn't want it any other way, Mrs. Holt." AJ scooted up on the bed, laying with her propped against the headboard. They sat together, each holding a son. She couldn't wait to begin their life together when they left the hospital.

The future was always an unknown, but with them beside her, her heart was shatterproof—no longer the glass heart it once was.

Epilogue

ONE YEAR LATER...

It was hard to believe the twins were already one. Alex and Colton had been the best gift life could give her—AJ, too. AJ and she were married at the courthouse before the boys were born, and they had promised his parents they would have a real wedding one day.

Well, they were getting their wish. Today, Jesse would walk down the aisle and marry the love of her life in front of everyone.

"Jess, you almost ready?" Allie placed her hand on her shoulder.

"You bet your ass she is... she wants to hurry up and get to the honeymoon!" Carmen shouted.

She had asked them to be the only members of her bridal party. Allie was her matron of honor, and Carmen was the only bridesmaid. Wearing a simple silk sheath, she tugged her dress over her belly. Beneath the silky fabric hid a secret she couldn't wait to tell AJ.

"Yes, I'm ready."

The music started, and Allie opened the door to the hall where she would marry AJ. Her brother appeared before her. "Sis, let's get you married... again." He winked.

She had asked him to give her away, which he gladly accepted. The wedding march started, and Allie and Carmen were already waiting for her at the end of the aisle. John guided her down the walkway toward her past, present, and future. AJ was handsome, dressed in a black and white tux. He smiled, eyes glistening with tears as he watched her step close to him. Taking his hand in hers, she barely heard the minister officiate the ceremony, lost in AJ's eyes.

"I now pronounce you man and wife again."

AJ leaned in, kissing her, staking his fierce claim on her. Everyone hooted and hollered in the background.

"I Love you, Mrs. Holt."

"I Love you, Mr. Holt."

The guests clapped as they walked down the aisle, hand in hand, toward the banquet hall. Everything was decked out in bright colors, and the music was already ramping up. They decided to forgo the traditional bride and groom dance and cake. Instead, they had an open bar, cupcakes, and finger foods. The guests were happy with that and had already started mingling.

"AJ," Alex approached them, "Congratulations again."

AJ shook his brother's hand. Alex looked off. He still showed signs of depression, and they were all worried. The only time he seemed ok was when he watched Alex. He was great with both their boys but had a special bond with Alex, seeing as he delivered him.

"Thanks, brother. You know," AJ smiled, "It's time you started living again, Alex. Get out there—find love for yourself."

"Nah," Alex looked her over, "I had my great love already."

He downed the beer he held in his hand. "You look beautiful, Jess. AJ, take care of her." He turned, leaving them to stare at the space he once stood.

"I wish he would find love. It would help him."

"I know, Jess, but we can't push him."

Don walked over, carrying Alex in his arms. "We are going to take these two little guys home. You guys have fun on your honeymoon. OK?" He leaned in, kissing her on the cheek.

She pulled Alex from his arms, wrapping him in a tight hug. "Mommy loves you. Be good for Pop-pop," handing him off to AJ, who hugged him. Betty came over, handing her Colton, whom she snuggled and kissed. Once they were done saying goodbye, they snuck out of the reception hall.

"So... Mrs. Holt, you want to grab some drinks with me and blow this joint?" AJ smirked as he spoke, his eyes twinkling with mischief.

"I will forgo the drink, but let's get out of here."

"Wait—you don't want a drink? Are you sick?"

AJ laughed. He knew how adamant she was about the open bar when they planned the wedding... she just hadn't expected a reason not to drink. "I am pretty sure drinking while pregnant is a no-no."

"Yeah, you're right.... WAIT—PREGNANT?"

His eyes were wide with wonder... instinctively, his hand went to her belly. "Yes—about six weeks." She eyed him, wondering what was going through his head. He swooped Jesse off her feet, spinning her around.

"I love you, Jess. This is the best gift you could ever give me." Setting her down, he pulled her flush against his chest. His lips found hers as he kissed her.

"Let's go home. I want to explore every new curve of your body. You think it's twins again?"

"God, I hope not..." She smiled. Her hand held in his as they walked towards the car.

Together, they would face anything.

Together, they would conquer the world.

Bound

BOOK TWO

SITTING UP, drenched in sweat, Alex reached for his phone. It was two in the morning, and sleep was no longer his friend. He might get a little shuteye if he was lucky before the nightmares invaded. It was the same thing, over and over. Being held prisoner was something he would live with forever. Even though he was home, his bare feet brushing the carpet reminding him he was free, in his mind, he wasn't.

Reaching for the bottle of water he kept bedside, he guzzled the remnants. This was the life he was destined for—bound by the terror he'd survived. He'd probably never be whole again. Stretching, he rose, untangling himself from the sheets wrapped around him. He went to the bathroom, slipping on a T-shirt and jeans from last night. He glanced at himself in the mirror.

Staring back at him was the shell of a man. The dusting of facial hair gave him a gruff, almost unapproachable look. His hair was still cut short, and he looked like he had his shit together—But if you looked hard enough, you'd see the broken man he was. Grunting, he brushed his teeth before slipping from the room.

He was heading out into the darkness of night to find comfort elsewhere. He had finally moved out of his parent's house. It took a year, but they decided he could finally manage his anger and could handle living alone. When he was rescued, he lived on base for the first year after his return. Returning to the life he'd left behind didn't work out for him. His then-wife, now sister-in-law, had buried him and moved on—she'd married his brother AJ. After two long years of therapy, he was living alone.

The small apartment he rented was in Campo, a few miles from his family. The Navy discharged him. While honorable, it was still a blow to his spirits. They cited him with several medals but stated his service with the SEAL team would place him under too much mental duress—a risk the military was not willing to take. While given the option of an administrative position, he opted for the discharge. There was no way he was taking a desk job in the Navy. Being a SEAL was all he knew.

Ironically, the only mental duress he felt was the lack of belonging to anything. He couldn't hold down a job–his specific set of skills left little to be desired by the outside world, so he bounced, doing odd jobs here and there. He still got a severance from the Navy—it paid just enough to cover his bills.

The first year back stateside was terrible—he'd be lying to himself if he said it was a smooth transition back to the land of the living. He'd lost everything. The woman he loved was married to his brother. She'd done exactly what he'd asked of her—move on and be happy. Of course, no one expected him to rise from the dead. Yet here he stood... alone.

Closing the door behind him, he inhaled the warm air. It was mid-June, and the temperature was anything but cold. He jogged down the steps, wandered into the parking lot, and found his bike. Straddling the smooth leather seat, he cranked the engine. The feel of the motor and the wind on his face were the only things that made him feel truly alive.

Pulling onto the street, he navigated himself towards the Grind. It was a local dive bar he'd frequented. Being in a small town, almost everyone knew him—hell, most of them grew up together. Parking near the front door, he noticed a rowdy group of bikers heading inside. Debating about going in, he mustered up his nerve and forced himself off his bike. Pulling the door open, the smell of old cigarettes and booze wafted through as he pushed inside. Catching the eye of Marty, the bartender, he gave him a curt nod.

"Hey, Marty. What's up with the crowd?" he said, ticking his head towards the obnoxiously loud men standing in the corner.

"They're from a town over, part of the 'Devil's Blood'—a local biker gang. Fraid' they may be trouble for us," he tapped an empty glass on the bar, "What are you doing out at this time of night? Nightmares again?"

Alex eyed the old man. He was former military, with ghosts of his own. "You could say that."

"Well, what'll you have? First one's on me, friend."

"Thanks, Marty... I'll take a whiskey. Neat." Marty nodded and walked off to pour his drink. Alcohol helped numb the emptiness he felt inside. His life was taken from him, the love of his life was in love with his brother—and now they had the cutest damn kids he'd ever seen. Everything sucked. Except for those boys. Jesse and AJ had twin sons a few months after he returned. It was a hard blow seeing them together, but the day he found her on the floor bleeding out, everything changed. He couldn't lose her, even if she weren't his. He delivered their first twin... whom they named after him.

Now, nearly eighteen months later, Alex was his little buddy. He loved both boys. Colton was just as lively and hysterical, but delivering Alex forged a special bond. Lost in thought, he sipped his drink.

"I said fuck off. I am not interested."

Glancing towards the end of the bar, his breath was stolen by the sheer beauty standing there. She was surrounded by a bunch of dirtbag bikers pawing at her as she stood her ground.

"Aw, come on, sexy. Just a little fun."

She wore a T-shirt and blue jeans, which did nothing to hide her stunning shape. The simple outfit hugged her curves like a glove. Her long red hair hung over her shoulder like molten lava. He couldn't take his eyes off her. His dick stirred, showing life for the first time in... well, forever.

Jesse, his ex-wife, was the last girl he'd felt something for—I hadn't been with anyone since coming home. It wasn't because his dick didn't work. Hell, he'd probably set a record for masturbating, but sex—nah, he didn't get turned on by anyone since Jesse... until now.

"Are you retarded or something? I said fuck off..." she huffed and gritted her teeth as she stared the sleaze ball in the eyes, "I. AM. NOT. INTERESTED!" She pushed past the beast of a man, only to have him grab her arm and halt her in her tracks.

"Hey—bitch... I don't take no for an answer."

He started rising from his stool, the protector in him screaming to flatten the asshole who had his hands on her. But before he could move to intervene, the crack of his nose resounded through the bar as if it were a branch cracking under the weight of a wild animal.

The biker covered his nose. "YOU. FUCKING. CUNT!! You broke my nose." He reached to grab her hand again. She was quicker, her fist contacting his throat, her knee burying itself into his groin—sending a man twice her size to the floor like a sack of potatoes.

The goddess turned, leaving the bewildered man in a heap on the floor. Alex stood with his mouth agape. She was fierce and didn't need his help, unable to take his eyes off her as she stormed towards the exit. She winked as she walked by him, her lips turned up in a half grin. Lost for words, he smiled and watched her beautiful backside exit the bar.

"Alex, you can stop drooling," Marty chuckled. "As for you fuckers—get out of my bar. I don't want your kind of trouble here. Next time, I'll call the cops. You understand?"

The group left, dragging their bloody friend out of the bar. Alex hurried to the door, making sure they didn't give the mystery girl any more trouble, only to find her tearing out of the parking lot on a sleek black bike of her own.

"Marty. Who was the girl... you know her? I've never seen her before."

"Yeah, I know her... and she ain't looking to be bothered. Best you keep that in mind, son."

Alex glanced at Marty, his eyes boring into him as his words registered slowly. Mystery girl left him wanting... more. Something he wasn't sure he was ready for, but he needed to find out who she was. He needed to see why his heart beat a little faster in only her presence.

"Sure... I was just curious," leaving the conversation there, "Thanks for the drink, Marty; I'll see you around."

"Hey—Alex," Marty hurried to the end of the bar, "Look, I know you're looking for work—I need some help around here. I know it's not what you're used to, but..."

Alex cut Marty off. Marty understood him on levels he couldn't even understand himself. "That would be great. I'll come by tomorrow—to sort out the details. Thanks, brother." Alex shook Marty's hand and exited the bar. He hurried to his bike, slipped into the seat, and cranked the engine. Racing home, he felt renewed. He didn't know if it was because Marty was giving him a chance... or if it was the vision of the redhead still making his heart race. Either way, he didn't care.

Once home, he locked his door and collapsed into bed. His eyes heavy with sleep, he prayed he could get a few hours without nightmares invading his rest. Slipping into the darkness of dreams, his vision was filled with a feisty redhead. Who was she, and where did she go? He hoped he'd see her again. Maybe Marty would share more details on who she was tomorrow.

Find out what happens when Alex finally runs into his mystery woman... and in the most shocking place of all!
Bound (Book Two)
Available on your favorite Ebook retailer.

About LC

Tattoos, whiskey, and bullets – where passion meets protection."

An International and USA Today Bestselling author, LC's an unapologetic down-home southern gal—with a bit of a dirty mouth who bleeds red, white, and blue. LC's never met a brooding hero she didn't love. She writes her men cut, tattooed, and tender for their down but not out ladies who need a little love from the right man. Her alpha heroes are less shades of gray and more shades of blue.

When she's not writing her hunky heroes, creating swoon-worthy love connections—you'll find LC curled up on the couch with a glass of peach crown and her very own sexy tattooed cop watching true crime on the television.

visit www.AuthorLCTaylor.com for more about

www.ingramcontent.com/pod-product-compliance
Lightning Source LLC
Chambersburg PA
CBHW060312310726
48976CB00007B/2300